Twisted Myths

A Quantum Book

Copyright © 2013 Quantum Publishing

First edition for North America and the Philippines published in 2013 by
Barron's Educational Series, Inc.

All inquiries should be addressed to:
Barron's Educational Series, Inc.
250 Wireless Boulevard
Hauppauge, New York 11788
WWW.BARRONSEDUC.COM

ISBN: 978-0-7641-6620-4

Library of Congress Control Number: 2013939131

This book is published and produced by
Quantum Books
6 Blundell Street
London N7 9BH

QUMTWML

Publisher: Sarah Bloxham
Managing Editor: Samantha Warrington
Assistant Editor: Jo Morley
Editorial Assistant: Ellen Bashford
Production Manager: Rohana Yusof
Author: Maura McHugh
http://splinister.com/
Illustrator: Jane Laurie, www.janelaurie.com
Design: Martin Stiff, www.amazing15.com

Date of Manufacture: July 2013
Printed in Huizhou, China by 1010 Printing International Ltd
9 8 7 6 5 4 3 2 1

Twisted Myths

Maura McHugh

Illustrated by
Jane Laurie

BARRON'S

Contents

Introduction

Myths are traditional stories that usually feature gods and goddesses, ancestral heroes and heroines, or semi-divine beings. These divinities are super-powered and can perform fantastic feats, but they are often prone to all the strengths and frailties of the human condition: compassion, jealousy, courage, vengeance, love, hate, tenderness, and fear. Thus, while the great sagas serve as entertaining stories, they were also designed to instruct the listener in the lessons of their age.

These narratives were malleable and changed depending upon the political regime, especially if an invading force held a technological advantage. It is easy for conquerors to change myths when they possess the only means for preserving and distributing it. Many of the myths we know today were transcribed by people who claimed to want to preserve information, but used the opportunity to add their own gloss to the original story—or to alter the mythology in a significant fashion.

Myths are not just exaggerated history or fantasy fiction, they tell us who we are, where we come from, and what we value. If one group deliberately changes the cultural narrative of another, they are potentially modifying the other group's identity.

Thus, we arrive at the challenge of examining ancient mythology, which started as an oral tradition and migrated into a written text. Those who wrote the myths down were often not the same people who originally told the story around a campfire or in front of a feasting hall. Like any story, myths evolve, especially in their early form when they were pure narrative imparted from person to person. Myths also affect other myths. People travel to different countries and cultures and bring their stories with them. Versions of the new story are adapted and folded into the host country's repertoire. Plus, there is always a person presenting the story, and storytellers above all wish to divert their audience. Authenticity can be sacrificed for the benefit of good tips from a paying crowd.

Quite soon you arrive at the quandary of trying to discover which is the best version of a myth to retell. Is it the oldest account, the most popular form, or the one that's been ignored? What makes one version better than another? There is no perfect answer to these questions. We can only begin to reconstruct myths from the point at which they were recorded, but they had a long life before that as an oral tradition.

As someone who is writing myths for a new audience, my primary aim is to express each myth in an accessible fashion, but also to hew as much as possible to the essential spirit of the original. Most myths contain a great deal of action and bloodshed, so I haven't had to "twist" the narratives to make them gorier—our ancestors had wonderful imaginations, and were capable of amazing invention. They also lived much tougher lives than we do today.

The more you read myths, the more you see the similarities across cultures. It's also startling, and reassuring, to note that despite huge social and technological advances, we still face the same dilemmas as our ancestors: siblings squabble, lovers are reckless, rulers want more power, and fate is fickle. Our ancestors wanted to be happy, just like us, and their stories impart that they were often their own worst enemies. Sometimes it is not the tribe next door you have to worry about, but the traitor by your own hearth.

When considering which stories to include in *Twisted Myths*, I tried to represent a varied selection from across the world. Many of the myths in this volume describe human dilemmas, but enacted by larger-than-life characters. Ishtar and Irkalla are not only powerful goddesses of different realms, but also sisters who cannot communicate with one another. Prometheus is a god who is punished by his insecure cousin for siding with the human race "against his own kind," and Pandora discovers hope in darkness. Izanagi has to accept the finality of death, and move on to embrace life. Balor doesn't want to lose power, so he takes steps to eliminate the threat, and in doing so, cements his own fate. The god Ra

unleashes blind revenge in the form of the goddess Sekhmet, but has to face up to the grim business it entails.

Then there are the fun stories, such as the various adventures of irrepressible Monkey, how Lord Ganesha gained his wisdom and lost his tusk, or the antics of the mischievous god Loki. Some of the myths are about a greater vision and mystery, such as Odin's search and sacrifice for knowledge, and the delivery of holy knowledge to the Lakota by White Buffalo Calf Woman.

There are also the origin stories, the ones that explain how people came into being, such as the myth of the five suns by the Aztecs, Pele's long journey with her siblings to Hawai'i, or the Voice, the Flood, and Turtle from the Caddo in North America. Plus, I've recounted a few adventure stories where gods or divine heroes battle to achieve their desires, such as Psyche's journey to Eros, the challenges Isis faces in the face of Set's treachery, and Nu Wa's desire the save her creation. Amaterasu discovers she cannot hide from her problems, King Elenre is forced to face up to his terrible decisions, and Māui risks much to impress others.

The twenty myths presented here are a mere sample of the rich narrative tradition we have inherited from our ancestors from around the globe. All storytelling today is built upon these sturdy foundation stones. These stories also demonstrate the diversity of human expression around the world, while reminding us of our similarities: we all require love, and struggle to understand our life's purpose. Myths reflect our perpetual occupation with these issues, and this is why they remain so popular and valuable today.

They first asked: who are we, and why do we exist?

Eros and Psyche

In ancient Greece, when gods and goddesses watched over the world from lofty Olympus, there lived a King and Queen in Crete who were blessed with three daughters: Xanthe, Melitta, and Psyche. Xanthe and Melitta were attractive, but the youngest, Psyche, possessed a beauty so radiant that it was whispered she was the incarnate form of Aphrodite, the goddess of love. By the age of sixteen, Psyche could no longer walk in the city without being followed by legions of admirers who threw flowers in her path, touched her garments, and begged for her blessing. Stories of her beauty spread to the neighboring islands, and across the sparkling sea to Greece. Day and night people lingered by the palace gates, hoping for a sight of her sweet face, assured it would bring them luck.

While Xanthe and Melitta shopped and met friends, Psyche had to remain at home. For years she witnessed her sisters return from their excursions, laughing and full of news. Alone in her room, Psyche's heart ached.

Worship at the temple of Aphrodite suffered. The people sent offerings to the fair Psyche who lived among them, rather than paying homage to an intangible goddess they had never seen. The sacrificial fires burned low. Prayers did not rise up to the heavens.

Eventually, Aphrodite heard of her mortal rival, and exploded into a rage. "How dare she claim to be my equal!" Her glorious features twisted into a dark visage. She clenched her fists and strode through the gilded halls of Olympus until she found her son Eros, lounging on a balcony.

Eros stood at his mother's entrance, and noted her angry mood. His wings flexed, and he gazed at the clear skies, certain he would wish to escape soon.

Aphrodite marched up to him. "My son, I have a task for you." He listened as she poured out her venom about Psyche. He had learned long ago to be still and wait out her storms.

"Shoot her with one of your gold arrows! Make her fall in love with an odious wretch—a man scorned and avoided. Let her passion for him bring her disgrace and ruin. When she withers in hated isolation, none shall call *her* Aphrodite!"

Eros knew he could not dissuade his mother, and besides, he was notorious for causing mischief with his arrows: gods

and humans alike had been humbled by his ability to inflict consuming love or aversion. So he agreed, took up his bow and quiver of arrows, extended his wings, and soared into the firmament.

That night, Psyche returned from Melitta's wedding. It had been a grand affair, with feasting, dancing, and singing. Despite her best intentions, Psyche had attracted more attention than was desirable during her sister's nuptials. Melitta wasn't pleased. Psyche noticed her sisters' animated conversation behind cups of wine, and the sour looks cast at her. Xanthe had married the previous year, and now they were the respectable matrons.

For all the admiration Psyche received, it was at a distance. She inspired awe and devotion, but men did not woo her. Psyche felt like a beautiful statue that people wanted to gaze upon, but not love. Her heart became marble in her chest, and Psyche wondered if the reason for her lack of suitors was because she could not inspire love, or feel it.

She lay in her bed, weighed down by despair.

Later, as she slept, Eros entered her bed chamber, for there are few barriers a god can't overcome. He notched his bow as he approached Psyche's bed. Yet, when he saw her face he faltered. As a god, living among luminous divinities, it was not often he was surprised by beauty. It was not just her charms that made him pause. In sleep she exhibited a soft vulnerability. Used to the strength and arrogance of his family, her face was like a drink of clear water.

For the first time his hand slipped, and his arrow fell. Unthinking, Eros grabbed for it, and its gold edge scraped his palm. He glanced at Psyche, and the full force of love's passion crashed into him. In that moment, he finally felt pity for all the lovers he had inflamed over the centuries. Overwhelmed, Eros backed out of the room, and shot into the night sky, desperate to cool the fever in his blood.

Psyche's unhappiness had not gone unnoticed by her parents. After Melitta's wedding they traveled to consult Pythia, the great oracle of the God Apollo at Delphi, about a suitable candidate for Psyche's hand.

The Priestess of Delphi looked up from her scrying bowl, her eyes black with dreadful knowledge, and made her pronouncement: Psyche could not marry a mortal man. She was to be taken to the top of Mount Ida on Crete, and sacrificed to a giant winged serpent.

The news shocked the palace. At first Psyche's parents resisted, and denied what they were told. Everyone was surprised at Psyche's reaction: she smiled sadly, and bowed her head. On the appointed day, Psyche dressed in funeral gray with an ashen veil, and walked upright in the hot sun before the drummers and a wailing procession. Their cries and laments echoed around the mountain.

Near the top, she kissed her sobbing parents and turned them away, along with the crowd. Psyche climbed alone to the peak of Mount Ida, and waited, trembling, for her fate.

When a warm gust of wind swirled around her, Psyche

thought it heralded the beast's attack. She scanned the azure skies, but detected no sign of the monster. Her dress fluttered, and a soft voice told her to be at peace. Zephyrus, the God of the West Wind, lifted her in the air. Psyche sped through the sky, her heart hammering and her veil whipping around her head.

After a time she landed gently in a meadow high in another mountain. A divine palace lay before her, made of white marble and with gold columns. Psyche walked through the fragrant grass to the building. Tiled mosaics studded with jewels covered the floor, citron wood panelling decorated the walls, and everywhere she looked, opulent gold caught the light. Women's voices in the air spoke to her, welcoming her as mistress of the palace. At first she was afraid, but they said they were her servants. They soothed her with music, led her to a bath, and then to a delicious feast. At no point did she see anyone. All the while the voices told her that their master would arrive after nightfall.

When she grew weary the voices guided her to a spacious bedroom, and she lay down to rest. As she drifted in a half-sleep a man's voice said, "Dearest Psyche, awake now."

She started up, fearful. The room was dark, but she could feel the weight of the man on the bed beside her. He spoke to Psyche for a long time, telling her how much he loved and valued her. At first she merely listened, half certain it was a dream, but thrilled by his words. Eventually he stroked her cheek, and whispered endearments. Quietly, she asked his name, but he said he could not tell her. She asked to see him, but he told her that his one requirement was that she could not see him until the time was right. Psyche pulled back from him at this, for it was a strange rule. He replied that he would give Psyche everything she ever wanted.

They talked for hours more, and Psyche told him things she had never said to another. Before dawn broke, he kissed

her and left in a rush of air.

The days continued with Psyche being cared for by her invisible servants. She spent her nights with her nameless suitor. He always left before daybreak. Soon they became husband and wife, and Psyche was content, except she missed her family. During the night all was well, but in the daytime, alone except for the voices, doubts and fears crept in. Her dreams were haunted by visions of her parents grieving, believing her dead.

Xanthe and Melitta, having heard of their sister's disappearance, visited their parents to console them. Their memories of their sister softened now they thought her dead, so they climbed to the top of Mount Ida to mourn for Psyche. Their cries carried on the wind to Psyche in her palace. Upset at her sisters' unnecessary pain, she called out to Zephyrus, and begged him to carry Xanthe and Melitta to her. He did as she bid, and within moments her sisters landed in the meadow, dishevelled and frightened.

It took some time for Psyche to calm her sisters and convince them she was not a specter. With a glad heart she brought them into her house for refreshments. The opulence and grandeur of her home silenced them and sparked old resentments. They asked Psyche about her husband, but her answers were evasive. After several questions they noticed inconsistencies.

Psyche left the room to find them gifts, and they spent the time grousing about their husbands, and how unjust it was that Psyche should secure such a marriage. Psyche returned with gold and jewels, and their envy deepened. With devilish cunning, they pestered Psyche until she admitted the truth about her husband, and revealed she was pregnant.

At once Xanthe and Melitta made awful suggestions about Psyche's husband. They claimed he was the serpent the oracle foretold, but transformed, and he would eat

Psyche and her baby when it was born. Xanthe said a ravenous serpent had been spotted in a nearby lake, and taking her sister's cue, Melitta confirmed the story and added embellishments of her own. They confused and unsettled Psyche so that all her memories of love became tinged with suspicion. In the light of day, everything that had happened at night seemed sinister and dangerous. They urged her to bring a knife and a lamp to bed, and when her husband slept to cut his throat. By the end of their visit Psyche's world was upside down. They departed, smiling, with the aid of Zephyrus.

Psyche hid the knife under her pillow, and left an oil lamp burning under a cover in the room. When her husband arrived, full of affection, Psyche melted into his embrace. Later, as she lay in the darkness with her hand on her belly, her sisters' poisonous words arose. Her hand slipped under the pillow and gripped the knife. She eased out of bed, uncovered the lamp, and tiptoed around the bed to gaze upon her husband.

He lay on his stomach, with his face to one side. His tousled blond hair curled over his cheeks, rosy with sleep. Snowy wings were closed across his back. One hand stretched toward Psyche's empty spot. At the bottom of the bed lay a bow and a quiver of arrows.

Amazed, Psyche put down her knife and examined the arrows. She touched the tip of one of the golden heads, and it pricked her. She yelped, and turned to look at her husband, whom she realized was the God Eros. A rush of passion and love suffused her. In her hurry to kiss her husband she stumbled, and hot oil from the lamp splashed across his shoulder.

Eros yelled and jumped up. He understood immediately what had happened. Psyche pressed against him, full of apologies. His face revealed his sorrow, but he said nothing.

Eros unfurled his wings and sailed toward the open window. Psyche grabbed onto his leg as he flew into the night, high above the ground. Her weight was too much for Eros to carry and he was forced down. He leaped into the top of a cypress tree, and Psyche tumbled to the ground. She cradled her hands over her belly, and looked up.

Eros glared at her from the swaying branches. "You broke my trust, Psyche. Our marriage cannot survive without it."

"Trust?" She staggered upright. "You didn't trust me with your name."

His expression was cold. "I disobeyed my mother's command to ruin your life, and instead I fell in love with you. I have sought to protect you from her jealousy by bringing you here, caring for you, and giving you everything you need."

Tears welled in Psyche's eyes. "Except honesty."

Eros gazed up at the stars. "Farewell!" He leaped, and within seconds he vanished from sight.

Psyche stood, her face lifted to the sky, until dawn. She walked stiffly into the house and rested. The following day she left her home, carrying provisions, jewels, and gold for her journey.

She did not know how to find Eros again, but she was determined to search until they were reunited. She traveled to one city after another, and visited every temple she could find. Eventually she arrived at the town in which her sister Xanthe lived. Psyche told her sister her woes, and Xanthe commiserated with her, while thinking she should seize the opportunity to secure the affections of a god. While Psyche was sleeping, Xanthe informed her husband that she had to travel to her parents, and she set out for Mount Ida. When she arrived, she climbed to the top, and cried out to Eros to take her as his wife, and for Zephyrus to carry her to him. Expecting all to happen as before, she leaped from the mountain. No wind caught her. She plunged screaming, and crashed onto the rocks.

Psyche continued her quest, with her baby growing bigger inside her, until she arrived at the village in which Melitta resided. Psyche detailed her difficulties to her sister, and as Melitta nodded in sympathy she remembered the marble and gold palace, now lying empty. She also stole away on a pretext and climbed Mount Ida, assured she could win over Eros. She declared her love, and ordered Zephyrus to bring her to her lord. She stepped off the mountain, but no airy grasp carried her aloft. Instead she fell, bashing off of the sharp outcrops until her body landed near the decaying remains of Xanthe, and scared off the crows. The birds soon returned to feast on the flesh of both sisters.

Meanwhile, Eros had returned to Mount Olympus to recover from his burn, but it was his separation from Psyche that caused him most pain. He pined in his chambers, thinking about his actions. The pride of a god is mighty, but his love for Psyche eroded it. Soon he cursed himself for his behavior, and considered how best to return to his beloved.

He had forgotten about Aphrodite. Since Psyche had left the house of Eros, with its protection from the gods' influence, it was not long before the news arrived in Olympus of the folly of Eros. Word reached Aphrodite's ears that her son had not cursed Psyche, but instead had set up home with her.

Her wrath shook the buildings of Olympus. She banged open the door to her son's rooms, and he stepped back in surprise. Her ensuing tirade covered her disappointment in him, and his disrespect of her. She threatened to remove his bow and arrows, and finally she locked him in. Then, she set her spies moving through the world to track down her son's lover.

Psyche continued her hunt for Eros, and stopped to pray for aid at every shrine or temple she found. The gods heard her prayers, but they were aware of Aphrodite's anger, and none wished to cross her.

One day, Psyche found a temple in disarray. Branches and leaves were strewn across the stone floor, sheaves of corn and barley were scattered about, and sickles lay abandoned. She spent the morning cleaning, not wishing any deity to be so disregarded. This place was appointed to Demeter, the goddess of farming, bounty, and the harvest. Her kind mother's heart softened as she witnessed Psyche, now heavily pregnant, cleaning her place of worship.

She appeared before Psyche, who bowed deeply. "Child," Demeter said as she raised Psyche up, "you have a grievous enemy in Aphrodite. She searches everywhere for you now, further angered by her son's betrayal."

Psyche asked, "How may I alleviate her fury? I wish only to be reunited with Eros."

Demeter considered, and remembered the pain she felt when she was sundered from her daughter Persephone, who was abducted by Pluto, the God of Hades. She looked at Psyche's belly and wondered what woman could ignore a grandchild. "Why not seek out Aphrodite voluntarily, with a contrite demeanor? No doubt she knows where Eros resides."

Psyche bent her head at Demeter's wisdom, but wondered if she could ever find mercy from a goddess who waged war on a mortal woman because of her beauty.

Demeter held out her hand, and Psyche took it. Within moments she was transported to a hallway in a wondrous palace. Demeter was nowhere to be seen. A cedar door carved with images of doves and flowers stood before her. She knocked.

One of Aphrodite's handmaidens answered the door, and she instantly recognized Psyche, for her mistress spoke of nothing else. "You!" she exclaimed. She grabbed a handful of Psyche's hair and dragged her into the lavish anteroom. "My lady," she called, without releasing Psyche, "we have a visitor."

Aphrodite emerged, and Psyche marveled at her dazzling beauty, even as she quaked in fear and pain. Aphrodite strode over to Psyche, and stared at her for a moment. Psyche felt hypnotized by Aphrodite's eyes, the color of the sparkling sea after a storm.

Aphrodite slapped Psyche across the face. "Finally, you deign to meet me, after a year of unlawful marriage to my son." She stepped back and sized Psyche up. "To think they compared you to me! Your bastard child has taken the bloom from your face." Psyche's hands immediately covered her large belly. "Don't think I'm delighted at the prospect of being a grandmother! You are nothing more than a kitchen maid compared to my son. I doubt you are even that useful."

She grabbed Psyche's arm and pulled her through hallways and into a storage room. Aphrodite kicked over sacks of beans, lentils, millet, barley, and poppy seeds so they mixed together in a large pile. "Separate those by this evening, or you will truly feel my fists." She slammed the door shut, and a key clunked in the lock.

Psyche collapsed on the floor. Her head and heart ached. The task was impossible. She allowed herself to cry in the darkness. Her baby kicked, and she sang a lullaby to it.

At the end of the song, a little voice piped up, "Psyche, do not worry. We will sort this mess for you." She looked down and an ant stood up on its rear legs and waved. A huge parade of ants flowed into the room from a crack in the floor and they began separating the grains and beans.

By the time Aphrodite returned, everything had been sorted into the correct bags. The Goddess of love inspected the work, and said nothing. She tossed a crust of bread at Psyche, and locked her in the room again. Psyche spent a cold, uncomfortable night, unaware that Eros was merely a few rooms away from where she lay.

In the following days, Aphrodite set Psyche a series of tasks, each guaranteed to cause her harm or ensure failure. Yet, each time she received advice from an ally who was touched by her plight. Psyche completed every ordeal. Aphrodite never thanked Psyche or praised her; instead she fumed and pondered a quest that would remove Psyche from the palace permanently, for she could not restrain Eros forever.

One day, Aphrodite slammed into the storage room where Psyche slept, and woke her roughly. "The stress of you ruining my son, and being a burden in my house has affected my complexion. Travel into Hades, and ask the Goddess Persephone for a drop of her beauty. She can spare it. Who sees her in that ghastly place but her tiresome husband and the legions of ghosts?"

Psyche paled. The Underworld was guarded and dangerous to the living; she did not know if being there would harm her unborn child. Aphrodite did not care. She turned Psyche out into the wild, and warned her not to return without a portion of Persephone's beauty.

Psyche wandered in the wild stunned by Aphrodite's request. After a while, she sat under the shade of a tree as the noon sun baked the earth. Her head dipped toward sleep when she heard a hiss, and a gentle rattle. She looked up to a snake with orange and black markings, coiled and rearing, by her side.

She held her breath. It flicked its tongue out, and said, "Psyche, I know your plight. I will tell you how to enter the Underworld and return." It then gave her directions and details for how to survive the hazardous journey.

Psyche thanked the serpent, and it slithered away. Then she offered a prayer to the Goddess Demeter, for the snake is one of her creatures.

When Psyche arrived at the entrance of Hades, her preparations were complete. She held a barley cake baked in sweet wine in each hand, and under her tongue were two obolos coins. She stepped onto the steep paths that led downward. She shivered because of the cold and the darkness, and the shades of the dead who whispered to her. Those lost souls lingered outside of Hades because they were unable to pay to cross the river Acheron.

Psyche kept her gaze locked forward, and dared not glance at what flitted at the extreme of her vision. She arrived at the bank of the river of pain, and waited. From the mist-shrouded water, a figure emerged: Charon, an ugly, cloaked man, poling a skiff.

Psyche followed the instructions she had been given and opened her mouth to reveal one of the coins. Charon's gnarled fingers removed it from her tongue. He gestured for her to enter the skiff, and they skimmed over the churning water. At one point the hands and face of a pallid, emaciated man lifted out of the river, and he gabbled at Psyche for aid. She said nothing, as she had been told, but his cries followed her for a long time.

She stepped off the skiff and approached the forbidding mansion of Persephone and Pluto. Standing before its great steps was the giant, three-headed dog, Cerberus, the hound of Hades. It raised its head and howled, whipping its scorpion tail, and shaking its mane of serpents. Psyche did not show any fear. She held out one of the barley cakes. Cerberus sniffed it, gently licked it from her hand, and loped off to enjoy his bribe.

Graceful Persephone greeted Psyche with kind words, offered a plump cushion to sit upon, and hearty food. Instead, Psyche sat at Persephone's feet on the granite floor, and accepted only plain bread. She imparted her mission to Persephone, who smiled warmly. "Even in my dread abode I have heard how Aphrodite taxes you for your love for Eros. It is all that is spoken of in Olympus." She left Psyche and returned with an ebony box. "This is what Aphrodite requires."

> The Underworld was guarded and dangerous to the living, she did not know if being there would harm her unborn child.

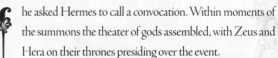

Psyche's eyes brimmed with tears of thanks, and after a long farewell, she left Persephone. She gave Cerberus another barley cake so she could reach Acheron safely, and Charon received another obolos to ferry Psyche over the river. From there, she walked up the long tunnel past its mournful phantoms until she was outside in the sun.

At this time, Eros had finally escaped his mother's prison, and was intent upon finding Psyche. He asked his fellow gods and goddesses if they knew where she was, and he discovered Aphrodite's latest test. Horrified at the prospect of losing Psyche to the Underworld, he flew at great speed to the entrance of Hades.

Psyche was elated by her success, and walked quickly to return to Aphrodite. Convinced she would see her husband soon, she stopped to fix her hair, and suddenly she wondered if Eros would still find her attractive. Her figure had swelled, and she had traveled so much and been tested so hard, that she imagined that he would be disappointed in her appearance. She regarded the box in her hands, and wondered if she could take a smidge of the beauty inside.

She lifted up the black lid.

Persephone had not placed any of her beauty inside the box. Instead she had placed the Stygian sleep of Hades. Its grains flew into Psyche's eyes, and fatigue overwhelmed her. She lay down, and fell into a coma.

Eros discovered his love lying in the grass and he feared the worst. He knelt beside her, but she would not respond to his entreaties. He lifted her head on his lap, and his tears fell on her face, where they washed the dust from her eyes.

She awoke to the sight of her beloved, and bliss returned. For a long time they held each other saying nothing because words could not describe their joy.

Eros was so enraptured that he lifted his wife into his arms, and flew with her to Mount Olympus. Once there,

he asked Hermes to call a convocation. Within moments of the summons the theater of gods assembled, with Zeus and Hera on their thrones presiding over the event.

Eros held the hand of Psyche, and declared, "This is my wife, my heart, my soul. We have suffered much apart, and none shall divide us again. We hope for your approval, but it is not necessary for our happiness."

The assembly broke into furious whispers at this bold statement. Aphrodite stepped forward, but Zeus raised his hand and all fell silent.

He glanced at Hera and she nodded. "Eros has played the matchmaker with many of us in the past, and we have suffered for it, sometimes pleasurably!" Laughter rippled through the crowd. "Now he has experienced that consuming love that will not be satisfied until one achieves its most blessed union."

Zeus stepped down from his throne, and Ganymedes walked to him with a golden goblet in his hands. Zeus handed it to Psyche. "Drink this ambrosia, and you will become a goddess. Your marriage to Eros will be eternal."

Psyche drank deeply. The gods cheered, and began a long night of celebrations.

Aphrodite made peace with her daughter-in-law, and since Psyche no longer resided on earth, the temples of the Goddess of Love returned to their previous splendor.

Psyche gave birth to a girl, and they named her Hedone.

They resided in love together, forever.

The Golden Apples of Idun

The gods and goddesses of the north live in Asgard, the best of the nine worlds connected by the ash tree Yggdrasil. It is ruled by Odin, the one-eyed King, who sits upon his high throne Hlidskjalf, where he can observe all people in all worlds.

At times, Odin grew tired of watching the action of others from afar and wished to explore the places he gazed upon. On one such occasion he called for sly Loki and just Hoenir to accompany him. The three gods put aside their shining armor, and dressed as men. They mounted their horses—Odin upon his eight-legged horse Sleipnir, which pawed the earth, eager to run. They galloped across Bifröst, the flaming rainbow bridge, and into Midgard, the world of men and women.

They rode through a green valley devoid of people, enjoyed the warmth of the sun, and admired the snow-tipped mountains on either side. After a time, Odin called for food. Loki and Hoenir glanced at each other, for neither had thought to pack provisions. At that moment, Loki spied a herd of muskox, with huge sloping horns, and thick shaggy coats.

"Watch this," he said. Loki seized his bow, sat up in his saddle, and let loose a shot. It pierced a muskox through the eye and shattered its brain. Its fall shook the earth and frightened off the remaining herd. Odin and Hoenir slapped Loki's back in congratulation.

Between the three of them they butchered the beast, collected branches of wood, and set up a campfire. They selected only the choicest cuts, and set them over the flames. Then they sat back to wait for the meat to cook, stomachs growling. After a time, Loki checked the meat, but it was still raw. They grumbled, but resigned themselves to wait. The sun sank another notch and he checked again, but the joints remained bloody and cold. The gods began quibbling until Odin heard another sound—a rustling in the branches of a nearby pine tree. He squinted upward. An enormous golden eagle, perched among the pine needles, watched them with bright, amber eyes.

"You're not having much luck cooking that meat," it noted.

The Golden Apples of Idun

Odin nodded. "And would you have anything to do with this?"

The eagle flapped its wings slightly, as if shrugging. "Give me some meat, and I am sure the rest will cook easily."

Odin agreed, over Loki's objections. Hoenir, as usual, remained quiet and observed the proceedings. The eagle flapped down and swooped low. Its large claws snatched most of the meat, and it started to lift back into the sky.

Loki leaped up, furious. He grabbed a long piece of wood from the pile of logs, and whacked it against the eagle's back.

Alas, Loki discovered the stick became welded to the eagle's back, and he could not let go of it. The eagle flew high away from the other gods, and Loki dangled from the stick, shouting and kicking.

The eagle zoomed through trees so their twigs tore at Loki's undefended face; then it skimmed close to the ground so his legs bounced off boulders and sliced through thorn bushes.

"Mercy," cried Loki, battered and bleeding.

The eagle turned its head and glared at Loki. "And what will you give me to spare your worthless hide?"

"Anything!"

"Good," the eagle replied. "I want your solemn oath that you will bring the goddess Idun and her golden apples out of Asgard to me."

Loki didn't reply, for Idun and her apples were the source of the gods' immortality and without them they would die. In that moment, Loki realized who the eagle really was; he could think of only one race who would wish this fate on the gods of Asgard.

"You're a giant," Loki stated.

The eagle screeched. "Thjassi is my name, and if you do not agree your remaining skin will be flayed off your bones."

After another beating, Loki gave up and swore to bring Idun to Thjassi.

Thjassi flew toward Odin and Hoenir and dumped Loki nearby. Loki limped out of the forest to find his companions relaxed by the fire, their bellies full.

Odin's eye gleamed, but he suppressed a laugh at Loki's disheveled appearance. Hoenir burped. Loki discovered they had eaten everything.

"We didn't know how long you were going to dance with that bird," Odin said when Loki berated them.

Loki scowled at his fellow gods, and malice burned in his heart.

They climbed onto their horses and rode to Asgard, where Loki's Flight became the favorite tale among the gods for a time.

Loki's wife, Sigyn, cleaned his wounds, but Loki didn't pay attention to her kind words or tender ministrations, for he was hatching a plan.

On the day Thjassi appointed for Loki to bring him

Idun, the roguish god wandered by her garden. She sat in the grass, her embroidered dress pooled around her, making daisy chains. Beside Idun lay a basket of large, golden apples. Loki checked that her husband Bragi was not around, before he hailed her.

Idun lifted her lovely face, framed by wavy locks of fair hair, and smiled at Loki, for she was a guileless goddess, and kind to all.

He wore an excited demeanor as a veil to mask his cunning. "Idun, during my last escapade I discovered a tree growing apples that look superior in size and color to yours. Perhaps they bestow immortality like your apples."

Idun stood up, her eyes sparkling with excitement. "Take me to them!"

"Bring your apples, so we can compare them when we arrive at the tree." Idun gladly complied, and Loki offered his arm. Together they strolled across Bifröst.

As soon as they crossed into Midgard, Thjassi, wearing his eagle-plumage, dove at them, and snagged Idun.

She cried out to Loki, pleading that he save her, but Loki merely watched until she and the eagle became a dot in the cloudless sky. He knew Thjassi was bearing her away to Jotunheim, the land of the giants.

He returned to Asgard, and said nothing when Bragi raised the alarm about his wife's disappearance. The gods searched everywhere, and even when Odin climbed into Hlidskjalf's seat, he could not see her in any of the worlds. When his great ravens, Huginn and Muninn, returned from their daily survey of Midgard, they had no news of Idun.

Without the apples, the gods began to age. Their skin hung off their bones, their eyesight dimmed, and their memories faded. Before it advanced too far, Odin called for a meeting of the gods in the hall Gladsheim. All the gods and goddesses shuffled into the huge building, and Odin asked if anyone remembered when they last saw Idun. Many of them could no longer recall breakfast. Heimdall scratched his long, white beard, and furrowed his wrinkled brow.

He coughed, and spoke in a wheezy voice, "I recall looking out of the window of my castle, and noticing Loki lead Idun across Bifröst."

All heads turned to Loki, who widened his eyes in false innocence. The group was far too familiar with his tricks to believe his countenance. Odin tightened his gnarled grip on his spear known as Gungnir; forged by dwarves, it always hit its target, no matter how wily.

"Truth, Loki!" he bellowed.

Loki spread his hands, "I had no choice," he began, and related his story to the assembly. Odin's son, Thor, had to restrain Bragi by the end, and Loki edged closer to the door.

"You will undo this Loki," commanded Odin, "And

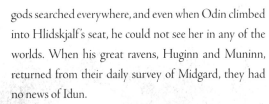

When his great ravens, Huginn and Muninn, returned from their daily survey of Midgard, they had no news of Idun.

return Idun, and our youth." The threat was not stated, but all knew that Odin was still capable of hefting Gungnir.

Loki narrowed his eyes, disliking the tone of the request, but already pondering the puzzle of it.

He sauntered to Freyja, who wore a veil because her famed beauty had withered. "Lend me your cloak, so I can retrieve Idun."

Odin nodded at Freyja, and Loki snatched the falcon-feathered cloak from her shoulders. As he did so he whispered to her, "You are so ugly now I wonder if any apple will restore your looks." Freyja made no reply, well used to the barbs of Loki, but under her veil, tears of dark gold ran down her shrunken cheeks.

Loki twirled the cloak around his body, and transformed into a falcon. He shot into the air, across Bifröst, and aimed for Jotunheim.

He arrived at Thjassi's keep, carved into the side of a mountain, and luck was with him: Thjassi and his daughter Skadi were out fishing on the sea. He flew into the building, and changed back into a god. Skulking stealthily was one of Loki's talents, so he discovered Idun's chamber without alerting any guards. Loki's pulse raced and his grin was wide, for he relished this kind of mission.

He slipped into the room, and Idun raised her tear-streaked face. Her expression hardened when she saw her rescuer. Loki raised a finger over his mouth, and Idun nodded.

Loki raised his arms, murmured spells, and traced runes in the air. With a pop, Idun transformed into a sparrow. He held the little bird in his palm and it trembled. He laughed at its rapid heartbeat, and carried her through the house until he spied an opening. Loki swirled the cloak, became a falcon again, and darted away from Jotunheim, with Idun in his claws.

Soon after, Thjassi and Skadi returned, holding nets and poles, and laden with fish. Thjassi sniffed the air when he crossed the threshold, and bolted to Idun's room. His roar of fury shook the mountain. By casting his own spells, Thjassi discovered Loki's betrayal. He pulled on his feathered cloak. In the blink of an eye he became an eagle, and dashed after Loki. Skadi tried to stop her father, but he was blind with anger.

Back in Asgard, Odin sat upon his throne and saw Loki beating his wings toward home, while behind him the dark shadow of Thjassi followed quickly.

He ordered all the gods and goddesses, and their servants, to take kindling and stack it upon the great wall surrounding Asgard. Puffing and groaning, the ancient deities did as they were bid and scrambled up the steps.

Now everyone could see Loki, striving to Asgard, and Thjassi fast behind. They cheered him on, and Loki put in a burst of speed. He arced over the wall, and Odin gave the order. The top of the wall burst into flames.

Thjassi, flying at full power, could not stop. He burst through the barrier of fire. His feathers blazed. He turned back into a giant, and plummeted into Asgard.

Weak as they were, the gods descended upon Thjassi, who lay smashed upon the ground, burned pink, and screaming. Thor raised his mighty hammer Mjölnir—deadly to giants—and caved in Thjassi's skull.

Silence returned, except for the panting of Thor, exhausted from lifting Mjölnir once.

Loki removed his cloak, and Freyja claimed it, for Loki was not renowned for returning what he borrowed. He muttered spells and drew runes, and Idun was restored. Bragi fell into her arms, hugging her close, and stroking her hair.

After a while, Idun went among the gods and goddesses and distributed her apples. By nightfall all were rejuvenated. They gathered in their feasting hall and held a marvelous banquet to celebrate Idun's return. By the end of the evening everyone was in a convivial mood

and many of the gods stood up to sing or recite epic sagas. Loki thought the mood too serious, so he led a goat into the room, cast his voice into the animal, and made such a series of jokes that the entire table of gods and goddesses cried with laughter.

The day ended in merriment, yet many never forgot how Loki endangered Asgard, and Loki came to believe that the assembly approved of him as a jester, but never as an equal.

These bitter seeds would eventually bring about all their ruin.

The Coming of the Tuatha Dé Dannan

When the world was younger, a dreadful flood rose up and swept away entire nations. When the waters receded, many lands lay empty. In the northwest, breaking the curling waves of the vast ocean, lay a green and verdant island devoid of any humans. At this time it was said you could travel from coast to coast on the isle without ever stepping out from under the shade of its ancient woodlands. The oak, hazel, and ash trees sheltered boar, wolves, and bears, and in the plains, wild cattle grazed on the sweet grass. Rumors of this abundant land lingered throughout the world, and when kingdoms rose again, leaders turned their thoughts west to its blessed shores.

So it was that distant relatives of the island's original settlers determined to move their entire population to that haven. They were called the Tuatha Dé Dannan, a race skilled in magic and warcraft. Their leader Nuada, a wise and valiant warrior, outlined plans for their immense undertaking. They abandoned their four cities, filled their flying ships with their people and their treasures, and set

off obscured by a mist.

On the first day of summer they landed upon a mountain on the west side of the island, and emerged to lay claim to it. As a mark of their determination, they broke their ships and burned them. Thick plumes of black smoke streaked the sky and heralded their coming.

Yet, they arrived too late. Another race of people known as the Fir Bolg, had already settled and claimed sovereignty over the land. The Tuatha Dé Dannan and the Fir Bolg had crossed paths in their previous homelands, and did not care for each other. The Tuatha Dé Dannan considered the Fir Bolg greedy and uncivilized, but although the Fir Bolg was an unruly tribe, they possessed shrewd leaders, and several among their people were as skilled in magic as the Tuatha Dé Dannan.

The leader of the Fir Bolg, Eochaidh mac Eric, had dreamed of a flock of black birds flying across the sea to roost on his island, and his *fili*—his chief poet—warned him that it was an invading force of magical heroes. So when the smoke from the Tuatha Dé Dannan's fires cast a gloom over the island, the Fir Bolg knew what it was.

Eochaidh sent his best warrior, Sreang, to parley with the Tuatha Dé Dannan. Sreang was a giant of a man, strong but nimble, and an expert in all weapons. He strode toward the encampment of the Tuatha Dé Dannan wearing his shield and sword, and carrying a fine spear. The watchmen spotted his approach, and Nuada ordered forth one of their best men, Breas, to meet the Fir Bolg champion. Breas was a charismatic and handsome man, and also an expert fighter. He stood before Sreang wearing his magical armor and armed with his best sword, and the two warriors took measure of each other.

They realized each other's heritage quickly, for they shared the same tongue. Breas asked for half the island for his people, and peace between them. Sreang scrutinized the armor and weapons of Breas, and noted the shining ranks of his fellow warriors, and was inclined to agree. Yet, Sreang was not a leader, so he bid Breas a courteous farewell and returned to relay their terms to Eochaidh. The Fir Bolg leaders held a convocation, and rejected sharing the land with the Tuatha Dé Dannan. "Once these people possess half," Eochaidh argued, "they will soon demand the whole." And so the Fir Bolg declared war.

The Tuatha Dé Dannan had been spying upon the proceedings with magic, and when they discovered that the Fir Bolg would not compromise, they moved to the plain of pillars, known as Magh Tuireadh, and built a fortified position against the mountain.

Among the Tuatha Dé Dannan there were three powerful women whose dreadful powers were feared by all. They were Badb, Crow of The Battlefield; Macha, The Bloody-handed, and most fearsome Mórrígu, The Phantom Queen. They gathered together and began raising terrible enchantments against the Fir Bolg. Black clouds boiled up and blotted out the sun, and from them emanated fiery hail and showers of blood that fell upon the Fir Bolg strongholds. It took three days before the Fir Bolg druids could counteract the potent spells. By that time, their people were discouraged and fearful, and their burned towns smelled like charnel houses. Despite this setback, Eochaidh rallied his soldiers and brought them to the plain of pillars where they set up their camp opposite the Tuatha Dé Dannan.

Through intermediaries they established their terms of war, and it wasn't until midsummer that the first day of battle dawned. Badb, Macha, and Mórrígu began their wails and enchantments, and across from them the druids of the Fir Bolg shouted spells and charms. The sound of the two armies clashing was like thunder, and the power of the warriors' strikes split the earth. For the first two days both armies were evenly matched. Every night the combatants returned to their camps and rested, and their physicians tended their wounds. Dian Céacht of the

Tuatha Dé Dannan was famous for his skill. Any injured person who was dipped into Dian Céacht's healing well would emerge cured and unscathed.

On the third day, Sreang strode through the combatants on the battlefield and defeated every fighter who stood against him. Muscles rippling and spear flying, he cut through the ranks of the Tuatha Dé Dannan until he confronted their leader, Nuada. Their battle was so swift and furious that few onlookers could follow their movements.

With a bone-shaking bellow, Sreang sliced off Nuada's arm at the shoulder, and the King of the Tuatha Dé Dannan collapsed into the grass, blood gushing from his wound. His attendants seized him, and dragged him to Dian Céacht.

Despite the injury to their leader, the next day the Tuatha Dé Dannan redoubled their efforts. This time, Eochaidh was cornered and slain. Bodies from both sides littered the field, providing food for the crows. Sreang now led a mere three hundred exhausted men. He realized to continue was folly, and petitioned for peace with the Tuatha Dé Dannan. They were so impressed with the fortitude and bravery of the Fir Bolg that they granted their enemy the pick of the five regions of the island for their home. The Fir Bolg chose Connacht, the land to the west, and all its islands.

The Tuatha Dé Dannan spread out and settled the other four provinces, and erected a great fort and feasting hall upon the Hill of Tara. Alas, due to his injury, Nuada had to surrender the rule of the Tuatha Dé Dannan, for only an unblemished person could be leader. The Tuatha Dé Dannan gathered at Tara and elected handsome Breas to be their king instead. Under the lights in the Hall of Tara, Breas glowed and raised a gold goblet to toast his people and their victory. He promised that if he ever let them down he would forfeit his leadership, and none gathered on that happy occasion ever imagined that such a prospect might come to pass.

At first, the Tuatha Dé Dannan prospered on the island, for the land was rich and bountiful. After a couple of years, a fierce, sea-faring race specializing in piracy saw the opportunity to fill their pockets with Tuatha Dé Dannan treasure. They were called the Fomhóire, and soon they bedeviled the new Tuatha Dé Dannan settlements—plundering and burning wherever they landed in their fast ships. Breas proved to be a poor negotiator, and within a short time, the Tuatha Dé Dannan were paying tribute to the Fomhóire to keep the sea-swift tyrants from their towns.

The chief of the Fomhóire was Balor of the Evil Eye. He lived in a glass tower on a spit of land off the coast, and from there he sent his ships to harry and steal from his neighbors. He got his name because one of his eyes had the power of death. The eye was sealed closed with an iron lid, but if he lifted it open by its ivory handle, any

> With a bone-shaking bellow, Sreang sliced off Nuada's arm at the shoulder.

living being in its path would wither and die instantly. He commanded the Fomhóire fleets and none dared stand before his deadly gaze.

Many years earlier, a druid had prophesied to Balor that his own grandson would cause his death. To prevent that from happening, he imprisoned his only daughter, Eithne, high in the tower, and banished all men from the property. Eithne lived a quiet life in the company of only women. Many nights she would lean upon the sill of her window and gaze out at the sliver sheen of the moon upon the ocean, and dream of escaping her father's prison.

As it often happens, Balor brought his doom upon himself.

Along the coast lived a hard-working Tuatha Dé Dannan known as Cian, who kept a farm with his two brothers. Cian specialized in raising cattle, and among his herd was a cow that provided milk all year round without fail. Many people tried to steal the prized cow from Cian, but he was far too wise and guarded her well. Eventually Balor heard about the marvelous beast and determined he would have her by any means.

One day when Cian was away from his farm, Balor tricked Cian's brothers into giving him the cow. He took the animal back to his island, confident that was the end of the matter.

Cian, however, had other plans.

He went up into the mountains and searched for a druid by the name of Biróg. She was known for her magic and craft, as well as having a hatred for Balor. For it was Biróg who had prophesied Balor's death. Balor had rewarded her insight by throwing her off his land without payment. She had brooded long on revenge, so when Cian asked for aid she was eager. She dressed Cian as a woman, and summoned a blast of wind that carried them across the water and onto Balor's island. Once there, she softly sang an enchantment to cast everyone on the island into a slumber—except her, Cian, and Eithne.

Eithne walked among the sleeping bodies of her companions, and tried to wake them. When she heard footsteps on the stairs she hurried to find out who it was. Eithne had never seen a young man before, and she was instantly smitten with Cian's solid frame and honest face. Until that moment, Cian was more interested in building up his farm than courting ladies, so he nearly stumbled when he saw Eithne's graceful form and delighted expression.

Biróg kept up her soothing tune for days, forgoing sleep and food, but never once letting the melody falter. During that time, Cian and Eithne fell deeply in love and pledged themselves to one another. Cian begged Eithne to run away with him, but Eithne was afraid to leave her father for fear of what he would do to Cian. Finally, Cian had to depart. He located his cow, and Biróg summoned the wind to carry the three of them back to the mainland, leaving Eithne behind. The people in the tower woke up, but the lingering effects of the spell made it so that no one noticed how much time had passed.

Eithne realized she was pregnant after a few months has passed, but she concealed her condition from her servants. When she went into confinement everyone found out the truth. Balor's fury rocked the tower.

When the baby boy was born, Balor ordered a servant to cast it into the sea. Eithne screamed and begged her father for mercy while her handmaidens restrained her in her bed. Wailing, the baby was carried to the top of the tower, and tossed over the edge. But Biróg was waiting, floating against the tower wall concealed by fog. She grabbed the baby, and shot back to the mainland to Cian.

Cian named the boy Lugh, and to keep him safe, he fostered the boy with Tailtiu, the greatest trainer of warriors in the five provinces. She fostered the sons of many Tuatha Dé Dannan families, so Lugh was raised with plenty of brothers. They grew up fast and lean, slept with their weapons, and bedded down in the stables with their horses, eager to leap up and ride into battle at the call of the trumpet. They were also taught blacksmithing and carpentry, how to compose poems and play instruments such as the harp. They were drilled with the genealogies and lore of their people, and they could recite every one from memory. The best students were also schooled in the secrets of magic.

> When the baby boy was born, Balor ordered a servant to cast it into the sea.

Lugh excelled in every category. Anything he decided to learn he would master at an extraordinary rate. Never had Tailtiu seen such a gifted student, so she worked him harder than any of her other foster sons. Lugh was given the nickname "long handed" from his brothers, for Lugh's arms were gangly, and his spear throws were pinpoint accurate from three miles. Yet, none of his brothers could maintain jealously against him, for Lugh was too good-natured and sincere.

As the new generation of Tuatha Dé Dannan grew up, the plight of their parents worsened. Breas proved to be a foolish leader only interested in his own comfort and gain. He increased the taxes so his people starved, and made the greatest of the Tuatha Dé Dannan people perform menial jobs for the Fomhóire.

As resentment among the Tuatha Dé Dannan increased, the physician Dian Céacht set himself a task: to create a new arm for Nuada, so he could once again qualify for kingship. After studying for years, Dian Céacht discovered how to forge a magical, silver arm. He fitted it on Nuada, and it worked with all the vigor of his missing limb. Yet, Dian Céacht's son, Miach believed he could do better. He cast more spells and gave Nuada potions, and after nine days skin grew up Nuada's arm and covered it completely. Soon Nuada's former dexterity returned, and he could snatch dandelion seeds from the breeze with his new fingers.

One night in the Hall of Tara, Breas ate and drank in luxury while women and children cried out in hunger outside. Witnessing the king's indifference to the plight of his people, the chief poet of Tara stood up and satirized his liege. There was no worse humiliation for a leader than to have his *fili* berate and deride him in verse. The poem was memorized by other poets, and within a short time it was repeated in every home throughout the land. Revolution stirred.

Nuada challenged Breas to give up the leadership of the Tuatha Dé Dannan as he had promised. Breas stalled Nuada, but secretly slipped away from Tara and headed straight for Balor's island. There, he requested an alliance with the chief. Balor accepted and made preparations for war. Nuada once again became leader of the Tuatha Dé Dannan, and warriors from the four provinces flocked to Tara to offer their services.

News of the forthcoming conflict swept across the land. Lugh was old enough to fight, so he packed up his armor and weapons and set off. After a long horse ride, he reached Tara at dusk, known by no one, sweaty and mud-splattered. The entire court of the Tuatha Dé Dannan was in the great hall, feasting and singing, to celebrate the return of Nuada. Lugh walked up to the two gatekeepers guarding the door and asked to be shown to the king.

"And who might you be?" demanded one of the guards with a sarcastic tone.

"I'm Lugh, son of Cian and Eithne, and foster-son of Tailtiu," he said with pride.

"Never heard of you!" the other guard snapped. "We're not letting a whelp like you in on this joyous day."

"Besides," the first guard added, eyeing up the young man with scepticism, "Only those skilled in an art are allowed into Tara."

Lugh folded his arms and said, "It's fortunate then that I am a carpenter."

"We have a master in carpentry among us already!"

"I am also a blacksmith."

At this the guards' eyebrows rose. "We have the foremost blacksmith in the land in Tara this night."

"I am a champion!"

The guards laughed for a bit. "All the champions of this age are squeezed into Tara right now. There is no room for a sly boaster like yourself in there."

And so it went on for a while, with Lugh recounting his abilities, and the guards disbelieving him.

Lugh grew frustrated and said, "Ask the king if any among his company is skilled in every art!"

"Ha," chuckled one guard, "You consider yourself an Illánach, the Master of all Arts! *That* I will impart to the king. I'm sure he will be *amazed*."

Inside the hot, noisy hall news of the strange young man came to Nuada's ears. He noticed two of his court playing a game of fidchell, and said to the guard, "Test him on fidchell, and we'll know soon enough if he has any strategy." The board and pieces were brought outside, but the guards could not beat Lugh. Soon, others came out of the hall to play a game with Lugh, but he defeated every opponent. When none remained to play against Lugh, Nuada called him into the hall. The room hushed, and Lugh described his lineage and talents to the assembly. The learned Ogma grunted in disbelief, and stomped over to the fireplace where an enormous flagstone lay, which had been pulled into the hall by a team of twenty-four oxen.

Ogma picked it up, muscles straining, and flung it at Lugh. Lugh caught it easily and threw it back at Ogma. The force of it knocked Ogma back, and his heels dug deep trenches in the hard-packed earthen floor. Then Lugh picked up a harp, and soon he had the entire hall roaring with laughter from his cheery songs, followed by tears from his heart-breaking ballads, and after that, he lulled them to sleep with a soothing melody. When Nuada woke up, he stepped down from his throne, and invited Lugh to take leadership for thirteen days. During that time, Lugh and the Tuatha Dé Dannan drew up their plans for battle against the Fomhóire.

Soon thereafter, a gang of tax collectors and their soldiers came to Tara seeking their annual tribute. They were well armed, and their demands for cattle and wheat were higher than the previous year. They curled their lips at Tara and its inhabitants, and expected them to accede to their demands as Breas had always done before.

Lugh answered their discourtesy by attacking the entire group single-handedly. He wore the golden breastplate of Manannan, which protected its wearer from wounds, and a helmet studded with flashing jewels. In his long arm he carried the relentless sword known as the Answerer—the sight of which was enough to reduce a warrior's strength to that of a baby. Within moments, the band had been cut down so only nine quivering fighters remained. Lugh ordered them to return to their master empty-handed, and to inform Balor that the Tuatha Dé Dannan would no longer pay taxes to the Fomhóire.

Balor did not take the news well. He consulted his druids, and discovered that Lugh was his grandson. His outward fury hid his fear, and he summoned his fleet of ships filled with his best fighters. He boarded the lead ship with Breas by his side, and they set sail for the mainland.

Smoke from burning towns heralded the arrival of the Fomhóire army. Nuada called forth all the Tuatha Dé Dannan warriors, poets, and druids, and urged them to use their wiles and skills to defeat the enemy. Then, the great host marched west to the plain of pillars, and took position against the Fomhóire for the second battle of Magh Tuireadh. Dian Céacht created another healing well and promised Nuada that any fighter—unless his head was struck off—would be completely healed after being submerged in its waters.

For several days, the armies stormed across the plain of pillars without either side gaining advantage. The Fomhóire marveled at how well the Tuatha Dé Dannan blacksmith kept supplying the troops with new weapons, and how the previous night's wounded would arrive on the battlefield the next morning, healed and eager to fight anew. During this time, Lugh had been kept from battle, for he was considered too valuable to lose.

But, on the fourth day of battle, Balor himself rolled onto the plain in his spiked war chariot and whipped his army into a frenzy. The Fomhóire druids rained terrible curses upon their enemy. In response, the entire force of the Tuatha Dé Dannan roared onto the field of battle, and the three women raced along with them shrieking spells and loosening their swords. Lugh was like a sun rising up from the east, and his luminous form blinded those who stood against him.

The earth rocked from the impact of the two armies colliding, and the ensuing savage fight was the bloodiest in memory. Wondrous heroes and powerful druids were slaughtered. Bodies piled up around Nuada and he could barely move his legs. Balor sped up to the king on his chariot, and flung his magical sword at Nuada. It screamed through the air trailing fire, and sliced off the king's head. An awful moan rose up from the Tuatha Dé Dannan, but in that moment, Lugh sprang forward to face his grandfather.

Balor knew his foe, and he reached up to lift the iron lid from his evil eye. Just as he swept up the covering, Lugh cast his red spear at the Fomhóire leader. The spear hit Balor so hard in his dreadful eye that it was driven halfway through his head, and knocked him to the ground. Even though Balor was dead, his eye was propped open by the spear, and its power of death remained. Its baleful gaze fell upon Balor's army and caused a path of devastation all the way to the ocean.

The Fomhóire army fled, leaving the Tuatha Dé Dannan to grieve their slain—even the clever art of Dian Céacht could not restore all who were injured.

Lugh found Biróg and they returned to the glass tower where he was born. There, he freed his mother Eithne from her long imprisonment. Their reunion was both joyful and tearful, for Lugh's father Cian had been killed in the recent battle. Lugh gave the glass tower to Biróg for her aid to his family, and returned to Tara with his mother.

At the height of summer, upon the Stone of Destiny at Tara, Lugh was named leader of the Tuatha Dé Dannan. The mighty race finally had their time of prosperity and peace on their emerald isle.

Until the next invasion.

Lord Ganesha

At the center of the world stands Mount Kailash, the huge black mountain whose summit is forever capped in snow. Its majesty is reflected by the six lesser mountains that surround it, forming a sacred lotus around the jewel of the snowy peaks. Upon its apex stands the ornate palace of Shiva, the auspicious one, and his twice-born wife Parvati. Shiva is both The Creator and The Destroyer, and when his tandava dance becomes so vigorous that it shakes the world, Parvati performs her lasya dance, and its graceful movements and serene power soothes Shiva. Then they laugh, and lie together in their sumptuous room.

Early in their marriage, Shiva had to leave Kailash to wage war with the other gods against a terrible foe. He dressed for battle, and lifted up his brilliant trishula—a magical trident that always hit its mark and severed any limb. Parvati bade her husband farewell, and walked through the rooms in her palace, now eerily quiet by the absence of Shiva and his army.

At the end of the day Parvati decided to enjoy a long, luxurious bath in preparation for the return of Shiva. After she disrobed, she smoothed sesame oil and paste on her skin, and then scraped it off her body along with the dirt of the day. As she got into the flow of the process Parvati contemplated the silence and emptiness of her home, and her desire for a child. The solution arose in her mind. She knelt and picked up the residue she had removed from her skin, and molded it into the shape of a boy. Parvati summoned her power of vitality, and poured some of it into the crude sculpture. Within moments, it grew and transformed into a beautiful boy, aged twelve.

"Ganesha, my son!" Parvati exclaimed in delight. She hugged and kissed him, and dressed him in gold silk. Then she gave him his first task. "Guard my door while I enjoy my bath. Let no one disturb me, no matter the circumstances."

Ganesha ran immediately to his post, delighted to be of service to his mother.

At the same time, Shiva returned from battle, victorious. He was covered in grime and gore, and wished nothing more than to embrace his wife, and wash off the dreadful stain of war.

He walked through the palace holding his trishula, which was streaked with blood. When he arrived at their chambers, he was startled by the strange, confident boy standing by the door.

"Who are you?" Shiva asked.

"I'm Ganesha, the guardian of Parvati. Who are you?"

Ordinarily Shiva might have been amused by Ganesha's bold tone, but after the burden of battle his good humor had departed.

"I'm her husband, arrogant child!" he shouted. "Let me pass, I wish to speak with her."

Ganesha put up his hand, palm outward. "No. My instructions are to allow no one to pass while my lady bathes."

Shiva's temper, still simmering from war, erupted anew. He swiped his trishula at the boy. The ever-eager weapon hummed and sliced through Ganesha's neck with such force that his head flew through the air, out of the window, and arced far away from Mount Kailash.

Parvati, alerted by the noise outside her chambers, jumped out of the bath, and opened the door. At the sight of her headless son covered in blood, and her husband standing over the body, she screamed so loudly that everyone in the world clutched at their heart in pain.

Parvati hunched over Ganesha's still form, and sobbed. Shiva's anger fled at the sight of his wife's anguish,

and he tried to soothe her.

She stood up, eyes flashing. "Shiva, you will revive Ganesha! You have the power to undo your terrible deed."

Shiva called for his servants to search the area for Ganesha's head while Parvati carried her son's body into her room to clean it.

Unfortunately, no one could find Ganesha's head, no matter where they searched. Shiva brought the bad news to his wife.

Parvati stood by Ganesha's body, and listened to her husband's report with an implacable, tear-stained face. "Hear me, Shiva, I will undo all that has been wrought in this world if you do not find a way to restore my son." In the tenor of her voice was the sound of destruction.

Shiva pleaded with Parvati not to repeat his mistake and take out anger against those who do not deserve it. Parvati agreed to assuage her vengeance only if Ganesha was brought back to life. Her son would thereafter be honored first among the gods, and his prayers uttered before all others.

Shiva agreed to his wife's terms, and called forth his celestial army, the Gana. He ordered them to go into the world, and to bring back the head of any creature that lay asleep facing north.

The Gana swept into the world, excited to carry out their master's command. Finally, a group of them discovered an old elephant that lay dying with his head facing north. They cut off his head and carried it back to Mount Kailash in triumph.

Shiva brought the elephant's head to where Ganesha lay, and fixed it upon his neck. Shiva channeled his magic into Parvati's son, and Ganesha sat up surprised. He flicked his big ears, and glanced down at the ivory tusks, and between them, his trunk. He sneaked his trunk into a bowl of sweet dumplings, snagged one, and popped it into his mouth. He laughed, with both a child's glee and the trumpet of an elephant. Shiva and Parvati embraced their child. Soon Ganesha was loved by everyone for his loyalty, good humor, and indomitable spirit.

As he grew up, Ganesha became one of the most popular gods among humans and gods, and collected one hundred and eight titles because of his heroic feats. He would become best known as the God of Wisdom and the Remover of Obstacles, as well as Ekadanta, Lord With One Tusk, because of two events that demonstrated his cleverness and strength of character.

Parvati gave birth to another son named Kartikeya, and she and Shiva were delighted to have two children. As the brothers grew up, they often clashed because of their different temperaments. Ganesha was happy and easy-going—unless provoked—and he loved sweet dumplings a little too much, as evidenced by his pot belly. Kartikeya was fast, quick-tempered, and enjoyed fighting. His favorite sport was teasing Ganesha about

> **Shiva brought the elephant's head to where Ganesha lay, and fixed it upon his neck.**

his ears, his trunk, or his fat belly. Kartikeya owned a huge, splendid peacock, and he often rode upon the bird's back. Ganesha's mount was a large brown mouse—which was actually the transformed god Kroncha—and this was another way for Kartikeya to mock Ganesha. He would start a fight with Ganesha, jump upon his sleek peacock, and snicker as Ganesha tried to catch up with him on poor Kroncha. Parvati and Shiva regularly had to intervene in the boys' arguments.

One day, a wise old man named Narada came to Mount Kailash, and was greeted warmly by Shiva and Parvati. Narada had a reputation for mischief, so the couple were wary whenever he made seemingly benign requests. At the end of their fine meal, Narada produced a mango, and claimed it was the fruit of knowledge. He offered it to Shiva, who glanced at his wife. She nodded, and he took a knife and prepared to cut the fruit in half to share it with her.

Narada coughed, and Shiva paused. "My Lord," the sage said with a twinkle in his eye, "the fruit cannot be shared, or it loses it power. It must be eaten whole by one person."

Shiva handed the mango to his wife, and said. "My love, please enjoy this."

Parvati regarded the fruit with suspicion, and refused the gift with the comment, "If I cannot share it with you I do not want it."

Lord Ganesha

At this moment Kartikeya and Ganesha burst into the room, bickering as usual. Ganesha, always hungry, noticed the mango and asked his mother for it. Kartikeya instantly declared he must have it. Within moments they were scrapping, and while Parvati separated them, Shiva glared at the old man. Narada shrugged.

After Parvati calmed the boys down she explained the mango was special and could not be shared. Shiva noticed Narada's amused expression at the stalemate, and he thought of a solution.

He suggested a competition to decide who would win the fruit. "Whoever can circle the world three times and return here first will have this mango."

Kartikeya laughed, assured of his victory,

and ran to his peacock. He jumped on the bird and they darted away to begin the long journey.

Ganesha watched his brother depart, and glanced at Kroncha. He could not beat his brother on these terms, but he knew his father was fair. He noticed Narada pat Shiva's hand and smile.

"Mother and father, will you stand up?" asked Ganesha. Parvati and Shiva got to their feet, and Ganesha walked around his parents three times.

"You are the mother and father of the universe, and my world. I have circled you three times as ordered."

Narada, Shiva, and Parvati burst out laughing, and awarded the mango to Ganesha for his strategy.

He waited for Kartikeya to return, and ate the mango as his brother sulked. All the knowledge of the universe passed from

the fruit into Ganesha, but more importantly, the Lord of Wisdom knew how to apply that knowledge in a cunning fashion to defeat any obstacle.

Yet, Ganesha was not above acting rashly when aggravated, which led to another one of his titles. When Ganesha was on the verge of adulthood, Shiva one day ordered his son to stand guard over his rooms while Shiva spent the day in meditation. It was a high honor, and Ganesha promised his father that he would not be interrupted.

Some time later, the warrior Parashurâma arrived at Mount Kailash. Parashurâma was a disciple of Shiva's, and had spent years praying to the god for a solution to the problem of the corrupt regime that ruled his native land. After many devotions, Parashurâma received the divine axe, Parashu, from Shiva. With this powerful weapon Parashurâma fought the dishonest rulers, and brought peace again to his realm. He embarked on a pilgrimage to Mount Kailash to thank Shiva personally, and after his arduous expedition, he was eager to meet his patron god.

He hurried to Shiva's rooms, and was surprised to see an elephant-headed man blocking his way in the hall. Brusquely, he ordered Ganesha to stand aside, but Ganesha refused without giving a reason. Neither of them liked the other's attitude, and soon they were quarreling loudly and fell to blows. Both of them were supremely talented fighters, and for a long time they kicked, punched, and threw each other around the hallway.

Then, Parashurâma unslung his great axe, and hurled it at Ganesha's head. As it raced through the air, Ganesha sensed it was imbued with the essence of his father, and decided he could not interrupt its path. He did not turn away from the blow, and accepted what would transpire. The blade hit one of Ganesha's tusks with a terrible crack. His tusk broke, and a large chunk of it fell to the ground. The axe bounced away and thumped against the door to Shiva's room.

At this, Shiva stormed out and demanded an explanation for their fight. Parashurâma discovered that Ganesha was Shiva's son, and apologized to both of them profusely. Never one to hold a grudge, Ganesha forgave Parashurâma easily and they became friends. From that point onward Ganesha's broken tusk reminded him of the importance of keeping a cool head. Wisdom and cleverness are easily foiled if one is easily provoked. Ganesha learned his lesson with good grace, and from it earned the trust and respect of Parashurâma and his father.

Lord Ganesha has one hundred and eight names in all, and each one tells a story.

Prometheus and Pandora

"**A**s you have overthrown me, so shall your children oust you," cursed Ouranos, the embodiment of the sky, as he lay dying before his son, Kronos. In his hand, Kronos held a magical sickle, which his mother Gaia had given him when she persuaded him to kill his father. The blood of Ouranos flowed scarlet off the cliffs of Mount Othrys, and dripped into the sea, which is part of the mother Gaia. When his fluids merged with her foaming water, new beings sprang into existence. First the giants emerged, already clad in armor and holding spears. They waded out of the waves, and their footsteps shook the land. Then the Erinyes burst from the sea and shot into the air—three winged women with snakes in their hair, and around their waists. Their eyes bled as they shrieked their fury, and all who heard them cowered, afraid of their maddening voices. After them, the Meliae swam to shore, kind maidens who would thereafter become the nymphs of the ash tree. Finally, the brine boiled up and the glorious goddess Aphrodite bobbed up to the surface. The current carried her gently to the shore, and when she stepped upon the sands, doves flocked to her and carried her to Mount Olympus, home to the next generation of gods.

Kronos sat upon the throne of Mount Othrys, triumphant, but as time passed the prediction of his fallen father grew to haunt him. When his wife, Rhea, became pregnant, Kronos was not jubilant. After she gave birth to Hestia he swallowed the baby girl entirely and held her inside his body. He did the same with their other children Demeter, Hera, Hades, and Poseidon, and Rhea despaired of ever seeing her offspring. When she became pregnant again she visited her mother Gaia, who advised Rhea to swap her baby for a stone wrapped in swaddling clothes when Kronos demanded it. Thus, the youngest god Zeus escaped the fate of his siblings. He was spirited away to a cave in Mount Ida in Crete, where his grandmother Gaia raised him in secret.

When Zeus was older, he traveled in disguise to his father's palace, and placed a purgative in the wine cup Kronos drank from nightly. Within moments Kronos was writhing on the floor in agony, and shortly disgorged his children. Kronos was too weak to do anything when Zeus sped into the room and escorted his brothers and sisters out of the palace. They fled to Mount Olympus, and met their cousins, including the clever and thoughtful Prometheus. He admired the ploy Zeus used to free his siblings, for Prometheus believed all problems were best solved through cunning and strategy.

Yet, there was no avoiding war with Kronos and the older gods, for they were enraged by Zeus' actions. To bolster their numbers, Zeus organized a daring raid on the prison in dreadful Tartaros, the pit in the darkest region of the underworld. There, he and his allies faced the jail's warden, Kampê, who had the face and torso of a woman, a dragon's body, and the tail of scorpion. After a terrible fight they slew Kampê, and Zeus freed the prisoners: the giants, the Hekatonkheires, and the Cyclopes. All of them agreed to join Zeus and his brethren in their battle against Kronos and his fellow Titans. As a sign of their thanks, the Cyclopes gifted Zeus with the power of the thunderbolt and lightning. Emboldened by this ability, Zeus began his assault upon the Titans, but he did not defeat them easily. It took a long ten years before the final outcome was decided.

Throughout that period it was Prometheus who offered the wisest counsel to Zeus on how to match the Titans in battle. Often, he recommended guile and subterfuge rather than outright attack. As the war dragged on, Prometheus became less and less enamored of the destruction being wrought in the world of the gods and the world of men. Unlike the other gods, Prometheus cared deeply for the fate of humans. While the gods and their allies raged and clashed, the lives of feeble men were disrupted by the aftereffects of their celestial wars. Prometheus had a hand in their creation, and had bestowed upon humans their ability to think and solve problems, to organize, and to ponder life's mysteries. He watched them struggle to feed and clothe themselves while coping with earthquakes and vicious storms brought on by the gods' clashes.

After a decade of destruction, the Olympians at last vanquished the Titans. Zeus threw many of them into the horrid prison pit of Tartaros. He personally clapped Kronos in chains, and left his father to spend eternity in darkness.

Afterward, Prometheus said, "As soon as Zeus sat upon the throne he assumed the haughty and imperious airs of Kronos. The son fought his father, only to become just like him."

Prometheus could not abide the arrogance of Zeus, and quickly grew into the habit of needling the new ruler whenever the opportunity arose. One day they were in the world of men about to witness a sacrifice they were making to the gods. Since the war ended the humans were flourishing. They had learned to build elegant homes, fine ships and chariots, and how to craft tools and weapons. Zeus observed this, but he did not delight in their inventiveness the way Prometheus did. What he saw was the potential for revolution.

The Titans had previously dictated that a proper sacrifice entailed killing and burning the entire beast—this was a costly exercise, and a waste of meat, which could be otherwise consumed. Prometheus also noted such sacrifices were difficult for those of limited means, who then risked the ire of their patron gods. He suggested to Zeus that they change the rules about how to propitiate favor with the gods, by only offering the choicest cuts of the animal as a burnt offering. To demonstrate, Prometheus slaughtered a bull while Zeus drank wine in the sun. He put the choicest cuts of meat inside the bull's stomach and left that on an altar. Then he took the animal's bones and hid them inside glistening fat, and laid them upon another altar. When Zeus was called to adjudicate, he wrinkled his nose at the creature's stomach, and chose instead the fatty offering.

Prometheus laughed, and showed Zeus his trick. From that point onward, humans could keep the best parts of the animal to consume, and the rest would be sacrificed to the gods. Zeus agreed to the change, but he was quietly furious at being shown up by Prometheus in front of men. In retribution, he removed fire from the world. All fires were extinguished, and no flint would

strike a spark. Zeus traveled back to Mount Olympus certain he had reminded Prometheus, and humans, who was in charge.

Prometheus fumed at Zeus' petty revenge, and decided he would return fire to humans. Without it they could not cook meat, keep warm, or forge tools. He crept quietly to the main hearth in Mount Olympus, careful not to draw the attention of Hestia, who kept the fire eternally lit. He stole burning coals, and carried them away in a hollow metal tube. After he returned to earth, Prometheus distributed the coals, and soon the fires on earth were rekindled. Since the fire originated from Hestia's own fireplace no god could extinguish it fully again.

The skies above Olympus roiled with thunder and blazed lightning when Zeus heard of Prometheus' treachery. He summoned the giants to drag up the thickest chains from Tartaros. Then, the giants overpowered Prometheus in his chambers, dragged him out into the vast courtyard, and manacled the god to weighty restraints. The other gods gathered to watch their cousin's punishment, but raised no complaint. Prometheus struggled to keep his head upright despite the fetters, for he would not bow his head to the tyranny of Zeus.

Zeus stood before Prometheus, and smiled. "Since you love the humans so much, I'm going to send them a special gift."

He snapped his fingers and Hephaestus, the crude god of smithing, pushed his way through the assembled

> When Zeus was called to adjudicate, he wrinkled his nose at the creature's stomach, and chose instead the fatty offering.

gods. He led a mortal woman of surpassing beauty, whose gaze was lifeless. At this time, there were no human women on earth, and no one died. Athena the huntress stepped forward and dressed the woman in a gown of silver fabric, an embroidered veil, and an ornate crown. Zeus approached her and touched her cheek. "My lovely Pandora, you will bring humanity's greatest gift: new life." He kissed her, and breathed a divine spark into her. Her eyes fluttered and awareness entered her mind. She stepped back, and looked around, confused.

Prometheus gritted his teeth, fearful for this innocent mortal, and expecting the worst from Zeus.

Zeus handed her an exquisite glass jar. "When you arrive at your new home, I wish you to open this and let the winds carry my blessing across the world."

Prometheus shouted, "No—," before a giant punched him. But in that moment, Prometheus released something of his divine essence as a protection for the woman. The act exhausted him, and he fell to his knees. Zeus took it as a sign of the chained god's dejection, but the ruler of Olympus was not through yet.

"Send her to Epimetheus, and explain she is a special gift to humanity." Hephaestus led the confused young woman away, and Zeus turned to Prometheus. "Your dolt of a brother will suspect nothing." Prometheus rose to his feet again, and strained against his bounds, but there was no breaking the chains of Tartaros.

Zeus raised his arm and a magnificent golden eagle screeched and swooped to land on his thick glove. "For your impertinence you will be chained to the peak of the Caucasus Mountain. Every day my eagle will rend open your chest and feast upon your liver. Every night you will be left alone for your flesh to heal and your immortal organ to regenerate. During the darkness you can contemplate the arrival of dawn, and the return of agony."

The eagle stared at Prometheus with its keen yellow eyes, and hissed in anticipation.

When the giants jostled Prometheus out of Olympus, and marched him to the mountain, he hoped Epimetheus would remember his warning: "Never accept a gift from Zeus."

But, simple Epimetheus was flattered by the attention from Zeus, and awed by Pandora's beauty. He gave her a chamber in his home, and his protection, and showed her the human world. The men who met her immediately loved her, for no one had met anyone like her before. Pandora exhibited a child's delight at the novelty of everything she saw. She accepted the flattery and attention as appropriate since it was all she knew, and everyone told her that she was unique, beautiful, and special. She believed them.

One day as she sat in sunshine in the garden of Epimetheus, watching butterflies alight upon flowers, she recalled the instruction from the ruler of Olympus.

She returned to her room, picked up the jar, and returned to the garden. She smiled, thinking how the

> Every night you will be left alone for your flesh to heal and your immortal organ to regenerate.

Prometheus and Pandora

world would benefit from the blessing of Zeus. She removed the stopper from the jar, and immediately a terrible revulsion shook her body. A ghastly smoke drifted out of the jar, and in its plume Pandora saw terrible images: pestilence, death, pain, sorrow, despair, lamenting, diseases, and weeping. She sobbed, doubled over at the realization she had unleashed this horror upon the world.

Her trembling hands dropped the jar and it smashed. She screamed when the awful fog engulfed her, and backed out of it, choking and retching. Pandora collapsed on the ground. All joy fled, and in its place ashen misery camped in her heart.

She lost her sense of time. A gray, dreary landscape surrounded her. Nothing would ever be the same again.

Yet, after a time, a small warm spot broke through the gloom in her mind. She sat up, and the sun warmed her tear-stained face. Butterflies danced patterns in front of her, ecstatic and oblivious to fear. Despite the knowledge of what had befallen the world, hope dawned in her heart. Pandora stood. She would not succumb to the curse of the gods. She would pledge herself to bringing hope to others despite their woes.

Across the world, high on a mountain, twilight brought respite to Prometheus. He lay bloodied and bound to rock, watching the great eagle fly away, knowing it would return.

A butterfly grazed his cheek, and fanned a little breeze across his skin. A tiny bubble of hope rose in his mind.

This is not forever, he swore to himself. I will be free. I will not submit.

He forced out a laugh in defiance of Zeus.

Maui Finds Death

When the world was young, death was unknown. On Aotearoa, the great island of two parts, there lived a couple named Taranga and Makeatutara, who had four boys and a girl. Makeatutara was much older than his wife, and by the birth of their fourth son he was slowing down. Many years later, Taranga discovered she was pregnant, but she was not pleased. Her husband was much weaker, and her boisterous sons were trouble enough. Taranga concealed her swelling belly under her luxurious cloak, unsure what she could do. Just when she could no longer hide her pregnancy, she felt the wrenching pangs of labor. She secretly went to a cave by the seashore, and gave birth to another boy.

Exhausted from childbirth, Taranga heaved herself onto her feet. She grabbed her obsidian knife, and hacked off her long, black hair. She wrapped the baby up in her hair, and threw him into the ocean. Shaking and ashen, she turned her back on his cries and walked slowly back to her village.

The ocean took pity on the boy. Long fronds of green kelp wrapped around him to keep him warm, and formed a raft beneath him. As he bobbed to the shore, the wind sang lullabies, and sea birds flew above as escorts, warding off predators.

Rangi, Father Sky, was gazing from the heavens at his wife Papa, Mother Earth, when he noticed the wailing baby, dripping with sea foam, on the beach. Mercy stirred in his heart, and he ordered the gods of the mountain peaks to carry the boy to his home in the sky.

Rangi named the child Māui, and raised the boy in his eternal home. Māui learned many secrets of the gods, and grew into a clever and powerful young man. He had differently colored eyes—one summer green, and one winter brown—and swirling tā moko designs cut into his face. Over time he grew discontented being the only human in the unchanging world of the gods.

One day he visited Rangi and asked about his parents. Father Sky noted Māui's determined expression, and knew that his adopted son would soon leave. He told Māui about his parents, and his birth. He also revealed that Māui

Māui Finds Death

had four brothers and a sister on earth. Māui asked to leave the heavens, and Rangi agreed on the condition that Māui teach the people of Aotearoa what he had learned during his stay with the gods.

Rangi called upon the winds to bear Māui down to the beach where his four brothers played a game of Niti. Māui asked to join in, and they agreed, not knowing who he was. When they saw his skill at the game, they asked his name, and he said, "I am Māui, son of Taranga."

The brothers threw their sticks down on the sand in anger. "We are the only sons of Taranga!"

"No, I am the youngest. I was flung into the sea at birth."

The brothers had never heard this story, and yelled that he was a liar. One of them ran off to fetch Taranga to repudiate the boy.

When she arrived she frowned at the stranger, and counted her sons loudly. "There are four here, and I have four sons," she said. "Go home, youngster."

Taranga turned to face her sons. "Why don't you practice your haka?" As the boys lined up to perform the ritual dance, Māui joined them.

The brothers shouted and pushed him away, but Māui stood firm, and stared at his mother. "You tossed me into the embrace of the waves moments after I was born," he said, and Taranga's eyes widened in shock. "I was rescued by blessed Rangi, and raised by the gods in the sky. Now I wish to live on earth among my family."

For a long while, Taranga said nothing, for shame and joy choked her. She had often regretted her actions, and was overwhelmed with gratitude to have another chance with her youngest son. She stepped forward and pressed her forehead and nose against Māui's forehead and nose in the traditional greeting. Māui's heart soared.

She brought Māui into her hut, and placed a finely woven mat beside her own mat, so they could sleep side by side. At first, Māui's brothers resented the attention Taranga lavished upon their new brother, but over time, Māui won them over because of the secret knowledge he had learned from the gods. He demonstrated how to make better pots to catch eels, the best way to craft a barbed spear, and a song to sing during the planting of sweet potato that would charm Papa into blessing the crop.

In the evenings Maui would entertain them by turning into different animals. Birds were his favorite. One time he transformed into a kererū, and strutted around with his white breast, glossy green head and wings, and scarlet eyes and feet. Taranga clapped and laughed. "*Now* you are handsome Māui! All who see you will love you."

One thing troubled him: every morning at dawn his mother slipped away from their hut and disappeared until the sun sank into the ocean. Māui asked his brothers where she went, but they could not tell him.

"How do we know she is safe?" Māui asked his brothers.

They shrugged. "She always returns."

"Don't you care where she goes?"

They snorted. "Care? Does she care for us? She is never around when we need her, and we rarely see our father. Rangi above sends us sun and rain for our crops which are nurtured by Papa in the earth. They are more father and mother to us. And to you."

This astonished Māui. He had longed for his mother when he was the lone human in the heavens, and now that they had reconciled, he could not imagine being so indifferent about her. He decided he would discover her secret.

That evening he ensured that the windows were blacked out completely, so Taranga would sleep late. Indeed it was well past dawn the next morning when she rose and left the hut in a hurry. Māui dressed quickly and shadowed his mother as she ran down a gully and stood before two large black boulders. Taranga checked that she was alone, as Māui ducked underneath huge ferns. Taranga then began to sing a chant, to which Māui memorized the words.

The rocks pushed apart and a dark tunnel revealed itself. When she walked inside, the boulders moved back silently to hide the way.

Māui stepped out from his cover and repeated his mother's words. The two rocks separated, revealing a dark chasm guarded by two vicious spirits with grotesque faces and tongues of flame. When they spotted Māui, a mortal

unknown to them, they gnashed their pointed teeth, slashed the air with their sharp claws, and hissed in rage. They rushed at Māui, but he turned himself into a kererū and flew deep into the tunnel. One of the spirits swiped at him with his tail as he darted by, but he only lost a couple of feathers.

Māui flew down the rocky passage and emerged in the Shades—a realm like the world above, but shrouded in perpetual twilight.

Men and women rested on grass under dull trees, and among the crowd, Māui spotted his mother sitting beside a frail, elderly man whom he guessed was his father.

Māui perched above them on a tree branch, hoping to overhear their conversation, but he was too far away. He plucked a wizened berry from the tree and dropped it on his father's wrinkled forehead.

Makeatutara cried "Ouch," touching his head, and looking up.

Taranga followed his gaze and narrowed her eyes, trying to peer through the gloom and the dry leaves. Māui's bright feathers gleamed even in the poor light, and he cooed softly. There were no birds in that desiccated world, and Taranga recognized his other form.

She stood up, and exclaimed, "It's Māui!"

Makeatutara was overjoyed to meet his youngest son, and he asked to sprinkle water over Māui, and perform a blessing of protection.

> In the evenings Māui would entertain them by turning into different animals. Birds were his favorite.

Taranga encouraged Māui, and told him it would offer him a defense against his coming challenges. She even claimed that when he came into his full power Māui would be capable of venturing into the realms of Hine-nui-te-pō, the Goddess of Death. "You could destroy her, and liberate humanity from her power."

Māui liked this vision of the future, and bowed his head so his father could bless him.

But his father's hand trembled, and his memory lapsed in the middle of the ritual, so he did not say the incantations properly. He lamented his mistake to Māui: "Forgive me for my imperfect blessing. You cannot face the Goddess Hine-nui-te-pō now. Stay with us in our eternal old age."

Māui patted his father's hand to comfort him, but Māui could not forget how his mother's face lit up when she encouraged him to conquer Hine-nui-te-pō. Māui knew his powers were great, but he decided to test and develop them to prepare himself for the encounter.

In the following years, Māui completed many outrageous feats, often with the help of his hapless brothers. Māui could charm anyone, and every new adventure was an opportunity to outdo his last quest. He snared the sun and made it travel more slowly; and he stole fire from its guardian spirit. He used the jawbone of his grandmother, who languished in the Shades, as a hook to draw up new land from beneath the ocean. On one occasion, he turned his brother-in-law into a dog, much to the annoyance of his sister.

Māui's people believed he was invincible. They created songs and dances to celebrate him, and over time their faith and conviction persuaded Māui that he could conquer any beast and complete any task. Yet, he aged just like everyone else, and when he imagined his abilities diminishing with age it sickened him.

He dreamed that he met Hine-nui-te-pō. He tried to convince the goddess that people should be like the moon: renewed every month by bathing in the Lake of the God Tāne. She disagreed. "People should die and become part of the soil." He woke up determined to rescue the dignity of humanity and destroy Hine-nui-te-pō.

Māui ventured back to the Shades to visit Makeatutara.

"I aim to destroy Hine-nui-te-pō," he said.

"Don't try that Māui," pleaded his father. "The Goddess of Death is too powerful."

"Don't worry," said Maui. "I have a plan! When she is asleep I shall jump into her mouth, take her heart, and bring it with me as I crawl out of her mouth again. She will die, and people will live forever."

"Anyone who goes into the jaws of Hine-nui-te-pō never returns!"

Māui frowned at this father's protests. "I made Te Ra the Sun God submit! How strong can she be?"

Makeatutara lowered his face. "Do what you will," he muttered.

Māui changed his tone. "Tell me where I can find Hine-nui-te-pō."

"They say the flashes of lightning on the purple horizon are the lights of her terrible eyes."

"What else?" prompted Māui.

"Her fangs, sharp as obsidian, are set in rows in a mouth like a barracuda's. From that deadly trap no person escapes."

"That's it?" Māui smiled. "I'm not afraid of that!"

He made his farewells, and his father wept.

His brothers refused to accompany Māui on his deadly mission. Instead, Māui called to his friends the birds, and many varieties of small birds flocked to him: the robin, the lark, the fantail, the white-head, and the rail, as well as many others. "We will go with you," they chirped.

Māui began his journey with the company of birds, and after many false trails, and wrong turns, he finally entered the abode of the Goddess of Death.

Her body was so immense that Māui could only see sections of it at a time. He walked carefully around to her head. The ground shook from her breaths, but he saw no lightning flashes, so he knew she was asleep.

He turned to the birds, and whispered, "Be quiet, and do not laugh."

"We will be silent, but please be careful, friend Māui," replied the birds.

Māui removed his fine flax cloak, and his tattoos gleamed on his skin.

He climbed up the goddess with the gentleness of a seed head tumbling over grass. He stood on her chest and stared at her enormous mouth. After a deep breath, Māui jumped head-first into the bladed mouth of Hine-nui-te-pō.

He got half-way down her throat, with his hands extended before him, ready to punch through to her heart. His feet and legs stuck out of the goddess's mouth, and the sight was so strange, and the birds were so nervous, that laughter bubbled up. They clamped their beaks tight, trying to hold in their terrified giggles, and not look at each other.

But the little fantail could not contain himself, and his merry laugh burst out.

Lightning flashed.

Hine-nui-te-pō woke up.

With a *snap* of her mighty jaws she cut Māui in half. Blood spurted from her monstrous mouth, and his severed legs tumbled to the ground before the horrified birds.

Shrieking, they flew away and told the world of Māui's death.

Māui's brothers mourned his passing. Māui had often annoyed them, but he had also pushed them to attempt new feats and share in his glorious escapades. They composed stories about his adventures, and passed them on to subsequent generations.

Māui died, but his fame continues to this day, and since then, every person who is born is fated to die.

The Patience of Isis

In ancient Egypt there were only three hundred and sixty one days in the year. During that period there were fewer gods; the mightiest among them was fiery Ra, who was pharaoh over the world; Thoth, the magician, wise and knowledgeable; Nut, the heavenly lady of the sky; and the lord of the earth, Geb. Ra became convinced that if Nut had children they would overthrow him, so he declared that none of her children could be born on any day of any year. Once Ra made a proclamation it became law, and Nut grieved, for she dearly wished to have children with her husband, Geb.

She sought out her brother, Thoth, and petitioned him for help. He pondered the puzzle, and then visited the white place of Khonshu, God of the moon. Khonshu was a young and attractive god who had a weakness for gambling, so Thoth easily persuaded Khonshu to play games of chance. The stakes were high for both, especially Khonshu, who wagered the light of the moon. Game after game turned out the same: luck remained on Thoth's side, for none could reckon numbers as well as him. At last, Khonshu conceded and refused to play against Thoth again. Thoth amassed all the light he had won from the moon god, and using his power he created another four days.

Thus, Nut was able to give birth to four children. On the first day Osiris was born, followed by Isis on the second day, Nephthys on the third, and on the last day, Set, who tore a hole in his mother's side upon his birth. Ra was furious when he discovered the trickery involved in the children's birth, and separated Nut and Geb for eternity. Thus, Nut gazes down upon her husband and children from the night sky where she is stretched over the vault of heaven, but she can never be reunited with them.

The young gods grew up quickly, and Osiris and Isis quickly gained a special place in the people's hearts. Yet, Isis never forgot it was Ra who had separated her from her mother, and she noticed how he watched her and Osiris constantly. Ra's immense power came from his secret name, which no one else knew, and which he guarded jealously. He was an older god, and at times when he was fatigued, his saliva slipped from his trembling lip and dripped upon the earth. One day Isis gathered up Ra's spit and kneaded it into clay to form a deadly hooded snake. It came alive, sparked by Ra's divine essence, and Isis set it upon Ra's path. Because it was formed from Ra, he did not sense it until the serpent struck his leg and poisoned him.

Ra fell down, his flesh burning, barely capable of speech, and shaking violently. He could not understand what was capable of hurting him. All the gods assembled around Ra's sickbed and tried to heal him, but nothing worked. At last, Isis stepped forward, for it was known she had the Breath of Life, and could heal all diseases.

She asked Ra for his secret name of power, and Ra told her all his titles known to men and gods. She did not reprove him, but mopped his sweating brow with a wet cloth. After a time, he screamed in pain, and Isis whispered to him, "Tell me your *secret name* so I can drive out the poison. I must call upon you truly for my magic to work."

Ra's skin flushed scarlet and his breath hitched in terrible wheezes. He ordered the other gods from the room, beckoned Isis closer, and gave up his secret name to her alone.

Elated, Isis cast her magic and infused it with the Word of Power. The poison obeyed the might of Ra's own name and became harmless. Ra's pain subsided, and he recovered swiftly. From that day forward Isis had power over Ra. Grudgingly, he retired from the throne, leaving it to the joint rule of Isis and Osiris.

The new King and Queen were generous with their gifts to their people. Wise Osiris taught men and women how to cultivate the vine, how to plant grain, and when to prune fruit trees. Luminous Isis trained people in the healing arts, spinning, and weaving. Under the tutelage of the gods, men and women transformed the dry plains into green and fertile lands. Together, Isis and Osiris ruled fairly from their palace in the vast city of Heliopolis, and peace was known throughout the country. Their uncle Thoth stayed close by them, adding his insight when necessary, and instructing men and women on how to write and figure numbers.

Set refused to live in Heliopolis. Instead, he created a home for himself deep in the scorching desert where no plant prospered, and Nephthys went with him.

Set resented his role as the youngest child, and his jealousy of Osiris's position and power was a smoking coal in his heart. It rivaled only his hatred of Isis. He often searched for ways to humiliate or destroy his brother, but Isis knew Set's spiteful nature, and guarded Osiris carefully against their brother's malice. But, Set plotted and plotted until he came up with a plan that he

was sure would result in the death of his brother.

First, Set obtained the exact measurements of Osiris by calculating the length of his brother's shadow. Then, Set invited his family to a fabulous banquet in his arid palace. Thoth, Isis, and Osiris arrived, and were led to comfortable seats with Set and Nephthys. Servants brought out platters of fragrant bread, meats, and spiced dates, along with clay jugs of beer. Isis refused alcohol as she wanted to keep watch over her brother, but everyone else indulged and soon they were all in good humor.

Sitting at one end of the room was a large chest, made from a variety of rich and costly woods, with intricate carving all over its surface. Eventually the conversation turned to its design, and everyone complimented its magnificent craftsmanship.

Set saluted their kind words with his cup of beer, and added, as if he had just come up with the idea, "Let us see if any of us can lie down flat inside of it. The person who is the best fit will receive the chest as a gift."

The gods thought this was a fine game, and Set stood up to demonstrate he was up for the challenge. He stepped inside the coffer and lay down, but his feet did not touch the far side. He jumped out, and waved in Thoth, who fared no better. Nephthys lay down inside the wooden chest next, but she was only half the required size. Isis was a close fit, but not perfect. After a lot of laughing and jesting, Osiris stepped into the chest and lay down.

> Distraught, Isis cut off her hair and tore at her clothes, and nothing Thoth or Nephthys said could comfort her.

It fit him exactly. Set clapped, as if delighted, but at that sound seventy-two attendants rushed into the banquet room from the shadows. Most of them formed a human wall around the chest, and protected the men who banged the lid shut, and hammered nails into it to fasten it. Osiris kicked against the lid and yelled for help. Two men, holding a vial of molten lead with tongs, dashed through the wall of soldiers and poured it along all the seams of the chest and sealed it airtight.

Isis, Thoth, and Nephthys cried out to Set, and desperately tried to break through the wall of men, but Set had spellbound the men to be impenetrable to the gods. Set's servants had moved so quickly, and with such coordination, that they had doomed Osiris within moments.

Then the seventy-two men lifted the chest—now Osiris's coffin—upon their shoulders and sprinted out of the palace into the darkness of the moonless night. Once outside, they split up into smaller groups and ran in different directions to confuse their pursuers. Set led the gang of men who carried the chest, and they made their way to the banks of the swift River Nile. They cast the chest into the water, and it floated downstream.

Disorientated, Isis, Thoth, and Nephthys wandered the whole night looking for Osiris, but it wasn't until dawn that they discovered the deep footprints leading to the river. At that point the chest had been carried far away and out to sea.

The Patience of Isis

Distraught, Isis cut off her hair and tore at her clothes, and nothing Thoth or Nephthys said could comfort her. Isis left them, and walked along the bank of the River Nile searching for the chest, weeping. Eventually she arrived at the mouth of the Nile, where it joined the Middle Sea, but there was no sign of the chest, and no one had seen it. Isis boarded a ship and sailed away from her homeland, into the world of strangers, seeking some indication of the final resting place of Osiris. Whenever she landed in a new country a group of children flocked to her, and helped her search.

The chest had washed upon the shore of Gebal, and ended up in a thicket of saplings. A Tamarisk tree, reacting to the divinity in the chest, lifted it up as it grew. Its branches cradled the chest and its bark spread around it until the chest was encased completely by the tree. Reacting to the blessed body of Osiris, the tree exuded a euphoric fragrance, and all that smelled it experienced peace and well-being. Soon the tree gained a reputation as a miraculous plant, and locals hung bells and garlands from its twigs. When word of its power reached the rulers of Gebal, King Melquart and Queen Astarte, they ordered the tree to be cut down. The branches were trimmed off, and the tree was carved into a decorative column for their infant son's bedroom, for Diktys was a sickly child. They believed the pleasant smell and its natural power would have a beneficial effect upon him.

After searching for years in other countries, Isis finally arrived in Gebal. As usual, she was greeted by a band of children. She questioned them about anything unusual, and heard the story about the unique tree with the wonderful fragrance. Isis suspected that the chest had been incorporated into the tree, and went to where it had stood. She knelt by its stump and inhaled what lingered of its scent. Tears drenched her face, for it was akin to standing beside her vanished husband. Isis kept her vigil by the tree stump for days, until reports reached the palace of a regal woman haunting the spot where the tree once grew.

Intrigued by the story, Astarte traveled with her handmaidens to seek out the stranger. She immediately fell into easy and comfortable conversation with Isis, and soon confided in Isis that her son, Diktys, failed to flourish.

At this, Isis, friend to all children, stood majestic and commanding, and said, "Bring me to your son." Awed at the power in the woman's voice, Astarte led Isis to her son's bedroom, where he lay, querulous and weak. Isis took him in her arms, and at once he calmed and cooed. "I will cure your son," Isis declared, "but in my own fashion, and none can gainsay me." Astarte agreed, and every night Isis shut herself in the boy's room, and every morning he emerged brighter and healthier.

Yet, Astarte's curiosity gnawed at her. No one knew what Isis did with her son in the evenings, so she decided she must find out. Astarte concealed herself in her son's room during the day, and waited. Right on schedule at dusk, Isis entered the room, and ordered the servants to leave. She barred the doors, and piled the logs up on the fireplace until the flames snapped up high and hungry. Then, she sat before the fire and formed a space between the blazing wood, into which she placed Diktys. In a blink of an eye, Isis transformed into a swallow, and she circled around the pillar containing her husband, and mourned him through birdsong.

Astarte shrieked, launched out of her hiding place, and snatched her son from the flames. He laughed in her arms, completely unscathed, and not even warm.

Isis shimmered back into her human form, and stood tall and threatening. "Foolish woman!" said Isis. "If you could have trusted me a few days longer all that is mortal in your son would have burned away. He would have been a god, eternal and forever young. Now, he will be long-lived, but mortal."

Queen Astarte realized she was in the presence of divinity. She knelt before Isis and called her husband King Melquart to join her in praising the goddess. They offered her riches and jewels, but that meant nothing to Isis. Instead she asked for the wooden pillar, and they were happy to gift it to her.

She ordered the column to be split apart, and inside lay the coffin that contained Osiris. Isis embraced it, and cried, for she had sought it for so long. King Melquart and Queen Astarte arranged for the chest to be carried from their palace, and they gave Isis passage on one of their best ships back to Egypt.

There, Isis brought the chest to a house known to none of her family, and after her many years of travels, opened it to look upon the face of Osiris. It was as if he was asleep. Isis spoke the words of transformation and her arms changed into wings. She beat them over his body, and leaned down and breathed into his mouth the depth of her love and the power of her magic, and Osiris opened his eyes and sat .up, restored by her beloved Isis.

For a time, the couple were happy together, alone in their joy at their reunion. Although their brother Set believed he had defeated Osiris, at this time he became strangely restless. Set rode out from his desert palace in his splendid chariot and hunted often, going to new places to kill ferocious beasts, yet it never satisfied the troublesome feeling in his heart. One evening he was returning from hunting when he happened to pass by the home of Isis and Osiris. Inexplicably, his horses reared and refused to continue, and Set dismounted and watched while his guards tried to persuade the animals to move.

Set noticed the light in the house, and out of boredom decided to inspect the dwelling. He walked through the

Isis boarded a ship and sailed away from her homeland, into the world of strangers.

courtyard full of lush plants and sweet smelling flowers, and his lip curled. He walked up the brick steps to the flat roof, where under a reed canopy Isis and Osiris lay asleep on a straw mattress.

For a moment Set could not move, but a white-hot fury flared up and broke his paralysis. His first action was to cast a spell that kept his sister in her slumber. Then he drew his sword and attacked Osiris like a frenzied beast. Set cut up his brother into fourteen pieces, took the chunks of flesh away with him, and scattered them all over the country. He was determined that Osiris would never rise again.

Isis woke the next morning to the sight of the blood of Osiris dripped all over her and the floor. She screamed in fright and horror, and cried out for Osiris, but he did not answer or come to her. She called to the birds of the area, and they gathered on the roof, and relayed what had transpired. Isis fell to her knees, grief and rage filling her equally.

She swore she would not allow her husband to suffer such an undignified end. Weary in body and spirit, she set out on the impossible task of finding every piece of Orisis' body. The birds of the marshes and the deserts, the mountains and the rivers, were her eyes and ears. They flew before her, guiding her to all the remote places in the land where spiteful Set had scattered her husband. For years she tracked down piece after piece with patience and dogged determination until she recovered all fourteen body parts.

She built a beautiful shrine of gold and lapis lazuli,

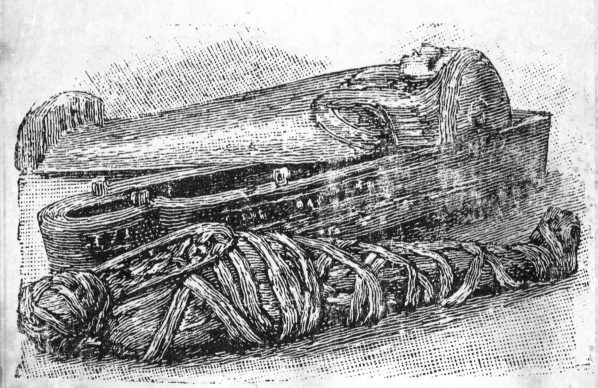

and reassembled the body of Osiris inside it. She summoned her magic like an iridescent cloth, and laid it upon Osiris. His body became whole again, but no matter what spell or incantation Isis uttered, she could not restore him to life.

She laid her arms over her husband's chest and wept. When she composed herself, Isis completed the proper funeral rites, embalmed his body, wrapped it in linen, and spoke the prayers to open the way for Osiris to enter the underworld.

Isis bowed down, exhausted by grief and despair, and heard Osiris speak, as if his mouth was close to her ear: *My love, I have gone on to Duat, the realm of the dead, where I am now Lord over all who reside here. You are not alone, for you will give birth to a son,* *called Horus. I will guide both of you in Spirit from my new domain, and together we will have revenge upon Set.*

Isis sat up, placed her hand upon her belly, and felt her baby kick.

She smiled despite her tears.

Ishtar Descends to the Underworld

Among the gods and goddesses of Babylon, there was none as glorious and furious as the goddess Ishtar. She presided over matters of love and passion, but she equally possessed the cunning strategy that warriors drew upon when they planned for battle. She committed herself impetuously and completely, to any project or person, but once her desire or the novelty wore off, she immediately searched for another entertainment. As Queen of Heaven she wielded great power, so few dared oppose her, but few could resist her seductions either.

The great love of her life was Tammuz, the handsome, charismatic god of the harvest. In him she found the one who understood her temperament, and could withstand her flighty nature. In her he discovered an equal in intelligence and appetite for life. Their desire for each other seemed endless. The world flourished when the divine couple were harmonious, and their sporadic fights shook the earth.

As Queen of Heaven, Ishtar knew all that happened upon the earth and the sea, for nothing could escape her view. Yet, her sister Irkalla ruled as the Queen of the Underworld—which was named Irkalla after her might—and Ishtar knew nothing of what happened in that realm. The sisters rarely communicated, and on either side lay jealousies. Ishtar disliked her sister's secrecy, and her power over the living—even the most vibrant creature withers and dies. Irkalla loathed Ishtar's dominion over the spheres of love and war—which brought mortal men and women to the door of the underworld most often. Both viewed the other as the source of the ills in the world.

Yet, when the news arrived to Ishtar that her sister had married the fire god Nergal, she was both affronted and surprised. She had not been invited to the wedding, and as the goddess of love and unions it was unthinkable that she should be ignored by her own sister. Plus, Nergal had notoriously wooed Irkalla and then abandoned her. However, he had eaten food in her domain, which doomed him to stay there forever. When he tricked his

way out of the underworld, Irkalla petitioned the triad of supreme gods, Anu, Ellil, and Ea, for his return. Irkalla intimated that she would raise all the dead who resided in her realm and unleash them upon the world if the gods did not agree to her request. The dead far outnumbered the living, and a contest between them was unthinkable. Nergal was ordered to return to Irkalla, and rumors abounded that he forced the Queen of the Underworld to marry him in retribution for condemning him to her domain.

Ishtar gathered her indignation about her like the blazing rays of the sun, and impulsively decided to visit her sister. She paid no thought to the fact that none returned from the road to Irkalla, or that those that resided there ate only dust and mud, and abided in constant darkness. As the Queen of Heaven, and commander of love and war, Ishtar rarely had to consider the consequences of her actions. She could charm or battle her way out of anything. Without discussing it with Tammuz, she put on her finest garments and attributes of power, and descended to the first gate of Irkalla.

The massive door to the underworld was sealed and its lintel was coated with dust. Ishtar stamped her foot and the earth trembled. The dust jumped.

She cried out, "Gatekeeper, open this door now! I am Ishtar, the Queen of Heaven, and if you do not comply I will shatter the door and its posts, and the dead shall be released into the world."

The gatekeeper called out, "Desist Lady Ishtar! I shall go to Queen Irkalla and tell her you are upon her threshold. I will return shortly with her reply."

Tapping her foot, Ishtar agreed, and the gatekeeper scurried through the gates of the underworld until he found his mistress upon her elaborate throne, with Nergal by her side. He groveled before her and repeated Ishtar's order.

Irkalla's face flushed crimson and her lips darkened with rage. "She dares command me in my realm! She may have her way in her bright domain, but now she will discover what it's like to venture into the world of dust and decay, which is under my absolute control!"

She nodded at the quivering gatekeeper. "Allow her passage, but she is subject to the usual rules. Treat her as you would any other traveling to my judgment."

At this, the gatekeeper grinned and hurried back to carry out Irkalla's command.

He opened the door and bowed low to the fair Ishtar. "Enter, my lady," he said. "Your sister eagerly awaits you."

Ishtar nodded imperiously at him as she swept through the entrance to the underworld. The door clanged shut behind her, and a gloom descended.

The gatekeeper reached up and removed Ishtar's crown.

The Queen of Heaven bridled at his impertinence,

but an unfamiliar weakness ran through her. Instead of blasting the man, she watched him put the crown upon a pile of other garments by the door.

"Why did you take my crown?" she asked, and to her ears her voice lacked its usual confidence.

The gatekeeper had seen this change millions of times, but never had he witnessed someone so powerful being brought to a humble realization. "It is the rule of the underworld," he replied. "All the trappings of the outside world are removed, until the essentials remain. Only then can Irkalla judge your worth truly."

A tremor of trepidation shook Ishtar, but she did not dwell upon it and followed the gatekeeper down the winding path until they came to a second gate.

He produced a large iron key from a ring of keys hanging from his belt, and unlocked the vast door. It swung open silently, and after he had locked it again, the gatekeeper reached up and removed the gold earrings from Ishtar's ears.

Again, Ishtar felt unable to prevent him from doing so, and when she queried him, he explained, "It is the rule of the underworld. All are subject to it."

The light dimmed further as they walked toward the next gate. When they were on the other side, the gatekeeper confiscated the thick chains around her neck.

Ishtar felt simultaneously lighter in body and heavier in spirit. After the fourth gate he took her ornamental

breastplate, and once they passed through the fifth gate, he unhooked the girdle of gemstones from her hips. When she passed beyond the sixth gate, he slipped off the clasps on her wrists and ankles. Every time she asked him why, he would offer the same explanation: "It is the rule of the underworld. All are subject to it."

They passed through the final gate, and at this, he removed Ishtar's fine robes, so she was entirely naked.

Ishtar was never ashamed of her body, but on this occasion she was consumed by embarrassment and anger. It was not the fact that she bared her flesh—she had done so in front of many others and reveled in it—but it was the method in which all the outward manifestations of her status and power had been stripped from her, and she had been made to feel as lowly as any ordinary person.

Ishtar noticed her sister sitting upon her high throne, dressed in cobweb lace and a crown of bones, and fury overtook the Queen of Heaven's previous lethargy. She flew at Irkalla, and her bare feet slapped against the black rock floor.

Irkalla leaned forward and smiled in triumph. Her joyless heart warmed at the sight of her sister's anger and subservience to Irkalla's rules. She snapped her fingers and Namtar, her loyal minister and messenger, appeared instantly beside her. Namtar was a tall, dreadful man, around whom hung a stench of festering rot.

Irkalla pointed a taloned finger at Ishtar, and said to

> **When she passed beyond the sixth gate, he slipped off the clasps on her wrists and ankles.**

him, "Take her to the lowest cell in my palace, and inflict upon her the sixty diseases you carry. Curse her with miseries on her eyes, her skin, her heart, her feet, her hands, and every part of her body! Let her be consumed with agony, and die in despair!"

Irkalla rose to her feet and spat out her final words, "Let mighty Ishtar become dust in Irkalla!"

Namtar disappeared and reappeared by Ishtar just as she reached the steps before Irkalla's high seat. He grabbed her wrists in an unbreakable grasp, and boils erupted across Ishtar's face. She screamed, high and shocked, for she had never experienced pain before. Her hair began to shed, and her hands became swollen red claws. Ishtar's body shriveled and wrinkled, her eyes shone milky from cataracts, and her spine shrank and doubled. Then Namtar and Ishtar disappeared. Yet, the Queen of Heaven's howls were heard from her cell in the distant dungeon for a long time, before they trailed off into moans.

But, without Ishtar in the world nothing was fertilized. No children were conceived, fruit would not grow, and love dwindled in the breasts of men and women, gods and goddesses. Apathy spread like a dull cloud, until few could rouse themselves to care or perform any tasks. Papsukkal, the vizier of the gods Anu, Ellil, and Ea, observed what was happening and began a search for Ishtar. Tammuz knew nothing about the whereabouts of

> He grabbed her wrists in an unbreakable grasp, and boils erupted across Ishtar's face.

his wife, and seemed strangely unmoved by her absence. Papsukkal inquired among humans and animals, and at last he discovered from the birds that Ishtar had gone into the underworld to talk with her sister.

Papsukkal donned mourning clothes, and rubbed soil into his hair. He went to the audience chamber of the gods, where the moon god Sin and the sun god Shamash spoke with their King Ea. They were perturbed by Papsukkal's appearance, and more so when they saw the tears in his eyes.

"My lords," he choked, "Ishtar is lost to us! She has descended to Irkalla!"

The gods immediately understood why the world had fallen into a dull languor, and Sin wailed, for Ishtar was his daughter. Ea knew that he could not allow Ishtar to remain in Irkalla, or it would bring about the ruin of gods and humans. He quieted Sin, and told the gods that he had a plan. He closed his eyes and created an image of a beautiful man in his mind, and breathed him into existence. Ea named him Asushunamir. He was luminous with beauty, charm, and wit, and combined all the best attributes of a man and a woman. Then Ea gave him his task: to descend to Irkalla, and trick the Queen of the Underworld to give him the waters of life, which she possessed. With that potent power Ishtar could be revived and brought back to full power.

Asushunamir made his way to Irkalla, and like Ishtar before him, was escorted through all seven gates until he stood naked in Irkalla's judging chamber. His spirit was guileless and fresh, and along with his novel beauty, Asushunamir bewitched Irkalla. She gave Nergal a task in the underworld to take him away, and ordered Namtar to set up a feast in her private chamber. She put new robes on Asushunamir, and sat him at a table piled high with fruits, meats, and jugs of wine. Ea had warned Asushunamir not to eat or drink while in the Underworld, so Asushunamir enchanted Irkalla with songs and dances, and pretended to partake of the banquet. He hid his food and poured away his wine instead. He constantly refilled Irkalla's cup so she became intoxicated within a short time. After a particularly exotic dance, Irkalla grabbed Asushunamir and pulled him close to her.

"I am told you possess the waters of life," he whispered in her ear. "Is that true, or is it just legend?"

She leered at him, and snapped her fingers. Namtar appeared by her side. "Fetch me the skin containing the waters of life!" she ordered Namtar, loudly.

Within moments, her servant returned with the water skin. But Irkalla's lids were heavy, and she had already forgotten what she had asked Namtar to do. When he vanished again Asushunamir sang a soothing melody to the Queen of the Underworld and within moments she had fallen asleep.

Asushunamir took the water skin, and moved stealthily through the palace and down to the dungeon. He located Ishtar's cell, and entered the darkness. She was a frail scrap of twisted skin and bones, and her breath was light and slow. He sprinkled the water of life upon her body, and within moments vitality and health returned to her. Asushunamir explained all that had transpired, and they carefully made their way up through the palace. Yet, Irkalla had sensed Ishtar's power as soon as it had returned, and the Queen of the Underworld shook off the effects of the alcohol. She waited for them in front of the seventh gate of the underworld, and glared at her sister and Asushunamir.

Since Ishtar had ingested the waters of life, Irkalla could no longer affect her, and the Queen of the Underworld had no wish to share her realm with her restored sister.

She could keep Asushunamir, but Irkalla chose to let him leave, and in retribution levied a terrible curse upon him: "I condemn you to eat only from the trash of the city, and drink from the dregs of the sewers! You will never know a restful hearth, and the besotted and the afflicted shall flock to you and harass you. This is my reward for your betrayal!"

She turned to her sister. "You may depart, but one must return in your place. I shall not be robbed of a denizen of my realm. If you can find no one, you will be condemned anew." Irkalla whistled a strange song, and a group of demons called the Anunnaki appeared.

She ordered them to accompany Ishtar into the world to make sure they returned with Ishtar, or her ransom-price.

Ishtar joined her hand with Asushunamir's, and squeezed it to give him strength. "You shall always be beloved to me," she whispered to him. "I cannot remove the curse, but I will change it. At the touch of your lips all your sustenance will become succulent and pure in your mouth, and for every person who turns against you, another two will aid you. You will always have my special protection."

Then the gatekeeper opened the seventh gate, and handed Ishtar and Asushunamir their clothing. They walked through the remaining six gates, and retrieved all of their valuables. Ishtar departed the underworld in her full regalia, and returned to authority.

When the outer gate to Irkalla boomed shut behind them, Ishtar inhaled a deep breath and threw her hands into the air. She laughed in delight, and at that sound, a lion roared and birds flew into the sky. Joy and fertility returned to the world.

Yet, the Anunnaki remained with Ishtar and Asushunamir, and she was constantly aware of their ghostly figures and cold presence. As she traveled back to the city of Uruk she gazed at the people she passed and considered if she could condemn them to Irkalla in her place. After being brought so low, Ishtar found it

When the outer gate to Irkalla boomed shut behind them, Ishtar inhaled a deep breath...

difficult to assign that fate to another. Her haughtiness had been rubbed off by the pain and loneliness she had experienced.

When they entered Ishtar's palace, the lovely Queen quickened her step, eager to find her lord Tammuz and be reunited with him. As she progressed, she noticed there were no signs of mourning. Servants looked startled at her appearance, and ran from her questions. At last she heard Tammuz's hearty laugh from the gardens, for there was nothing he liked better than to be outside among the verdant vegetation. It was also harvest time, which was special to him.

She moved through the lush ferns and sweetly scented flowers, and stopped still when she caught sight of her husband. He did not wear mourning clothes, but was dressed in his normal, colorful attire. With him was his sister Belili, and another woman. They were laughing together in a far too familiar fashion.

Fury boiled up in Ishtar and a wrathful light flashed in her eyes. She turned to the Anunnaki.

"I have chosen my replacement," she roared, and snapped around to face her husband. His eyes widened in shock and guilt. The two women froze at the sight of the goddess. She pointed at Tammuz, "Take him to Irkalla!"

The Anunnaki were by Tammuz's side immediately, and seized him in their freezing grasp.

"No, Ishtar, please!" Tammuz shouted.

It was too late. The Anunnaki rushed him from that place, and within moments he had vanished. The other woman disappeared as quickly, but Belili wept and pleaded with the goddess to change her mind, and spare her brother.

It was far too soon to appeal to the goddess's better nature. Ishtar shook off Belili and returned to her bed chamber, alone.

As Ishtar's temper cooled, she considered her decision in her mind. It had been made rashly, before she had questioned Tammuz. The rigors she had been subjected to in Irkalla had robbed her of her reserves, and Ishtar ruefully accepted that she was often quick to judge.

People mourned the loss of Tammuz, and Ishtar could not help wondering if they had displayed such affection for her when she was missing. The plants died, and the seasons turned cold and chilly. Little grew in the world with Tammuz locked up in Irkalla. Ishtar's presence in the world buoyed it up, but without Tammuz the pulse of life remained low.

At last, Belili arranged an audience with Ishtar and begged for clemency for her brother, Tammuz.

Ishtar sat on her throne, aware of the empty spot beside her. "It's too late, Belili," she said. "He was my ransom price. My sister must have her portion, and she will not return someone who has been allotted to her by right. Plus, she will not listen to reason from me."

Belili's expression was strained when she stammered, "How, how... about another substitution?"

Ishtar Descends to the Underworld

Ishtar raised an eyebrow. "I will not return to my sister's embrace a second time."

"I will go," she said, with an audible gulp.

Ishtar sized up Belili's strength and determination, and looked out her window at the garden. The trees were bare, and the grasses brown. She longed for green shoots and bright flowers.

She turned her gaze back upon Belili. "Six months," she said. "I will offer Irkalla to take you for six months of the year, and for Tammuz to reside in her place the other six months of the year."

Belili nodded as if not willing to trust herself to assent to the bargain.

"I'm sure Irkalla would prefer to have someone with less vigor in her dead realm some of the time.

It must be hard to endure the sense of the rising sap in a domain assigned to death. It must remind those who reside there what they miss."

Belili bowed her head, and Ishtar sent a messenger to her sister to offer her the deal.

In Irkalla, the Queen of the Underworld stepped upon a daisy growing up from a crack, and regretted the day Tammuz was sent to her domain.

The Fifth Sun

Since the beginning of time, four suns have come and gone in the Aztec sky. These suns mark the four worlds that were created and destroyed through the discontent and squabbles of the creator gods. This was not what the great divinity Ometeotl desired when he/she first emerged from chaos, and brought forth life from the emptiness. As the universe's first expression, Ometeotl contained both light and darkness, female and male, good and evil, and fire and water. He/she contained all potential, thus could manifest beings through thought and intention alone.

From Ometeotl emerged the four Tezcatlipocas, who were given dominion over each of the four cardinal directions. White Tezcatlipoca, also known as Quetzalcoatl, who was the god of light, mercy and wind, presided over the West. In the South, Blue Tezcatlipoca, referred to as Huitzilopochtli, the god of war, reigned. Red Tezcatlipoca, or Xipe Totec, ruled in the East, and his providence was gold, farming, and the spring. Black Tezcatlipoca camped up in the North, and he was only ever referred to in whispers as Tezcatlipoca, for his other name was secret. He was the god of night, deceit, and sorcery.

For six hundred years the Tezcatlipocas pondered their parent, the universe as it was manifested, and each other, until they arrived at a profound understanding of all that existed—and wished for something new. They sprang into a flurry of activity, and created a vast ocean, and the god Tlaloc to have dominion over the ocean and the rains. Within the ocean, they conjured a gargantuan beast named Cipactli, which was part crocodile and part fish, and it had a mouth at every joint. She had an appetite without end. Every new creature the four Tezcatlipocas created fell into the ocean, and Cipactli devoured them.

At last the gods realized they would have to destroy Cipactli, and they made war upon her. The immense monster was fast and strong, and at first they could not even get close to her. Then, Tezcatlipoca put his foot in the water as bait, and she could not resist the treat. Her giant jaws snapped upon Tezcatlipoca's foot, and the

other three gods each seized a corner of the enormous monster and pulled. Cipactli thrashed about and ripped off Tezcatlipoca's foot before she was torn asunder.

From the remains of the monster's body, the gods ordered the universe: Thirteen heavens were formed from Cipactli's head; the earth was hammered out from her torso; and the path to the nine underworlds, known as Mictlán, was the length of Cipactli's tail. From the spine of Cipactli, they fashioned the skeleton god Mictlantecuhtli and goddess Mictlancihuatl to be the King and Queen of the underworld—because after this, the Tezcatlipocas decided to create the first humans, who were destined to die eventually. After death, they would traverse the long road to Mictlán and face many trials before they secured their eternal rest in the underworld.

They had more uses from Cipactli: Her claws transformed into trees, grass and flowers sprouted from her scales, and her eyes liquidized and became the source of wells and springs. Her mouth transformed into vast rivers and echoing caves, and her shoulders were the mountains of earth. The gods also created the birds, animals, and fish from Cipactli's entrails. The goddess Xochiquetzal came into being, and she loved the plants and creatures as if they were her own children. Wherever she went, birds and butterflies followed her. Soon thereafter Tlaloc wooed her, and married her. During this period many other gods sprang up, such as the earth goddess Coatlicue, from whom the four hundred southern stars were born.

The first men and women created by the gods were giants, and were tasked with tending the earth and honoring it, for it was only through the death of Cipactli that they had a home. No sun shone above, and the gods realized that one among them would have to go into the sky and act as a sun to the earth. Tezcatlipoca volunteered,

and ascended to the sky, but because of his injury, the light he cast was pale and weak. Little flourished in the world, and the remaining gods watched in frustration as the creation they had labored over for so long struggled to exist.

One day Quetzalcoatl lost his temper, and threw his stone club at his brother in the sky. Tezcatlipoca unbalanced and tumbled from the heavens. The world was instantly plunged into darkness. In his fury at his brother's insult, Tezcatlipoca summoned jaguars and set them loose upon all the men and women in the world. Every human being was devoured.

Quetzalcoatl decided this was his opportunity to prove his worth. He summoned a fast wind, shot up into the sky, and became the new sun. The gods created more humans, and this time, they were the size of people today. For a time, all went well and Quetzalcoatl beamed down from the heavens, convinced he was doing a much better job than his brother. Yet, sulky Tezcatlipoca closely monitored the new human race, and believed they were becoming rude and uncivilized. He summoned his power and cast a spell that changed them into monkeys. Enraged at his brother's meddling, Quetzalcoatl called forth a huge hurricane. It howled across the world, and blasted the chattering monkeys off the surface.

With no people to watch over, Quetzalcoatl abdicated as sun, and once again, darkness descended upon the earth. The gods recreated people for the third time, and Tlaloc volunteered for the honor as the sun, much to the annoyance of fair Xochiquetzal, who was left on her own to watch her husband traverse the sky every day. She busied herself tending fields and treating animals to distract herself from her loneliness. Tezcatlipoca admired her beauty and grace, and pretended to have an interest in her flowers and birds in order to get close to her. When she was unguarded, he abducted her, brought her to his palace, and forced her to marry him.

High up in the sky Tlaloc watched this terrible tragedy unfold, and his light brightened with fury. Plants withered, and the people were beaten down by Tlaloc's fierce heat. They petitioned him to send rain, since he was also the god of water. He refused to summon the nourishing rain, and instead increased the fury of his heat. More and more the people cried out for mercy, but it only infuriated him further. He looked down upon Tezcatlipoca and Xochiquetzal in their home together and hatred consumed him. The next time he heard the pleas of the mortals for rain, Tlaloc poured a rain of fire upon them. In this fashion, the third world burned up and all life was destroyed.

Tlaloc descended from the sky and walked among the ashes of the world. At this time he beheld the goddess Chalchiuhtlicue, who was attempting to summon water to revive part of creation. As a goddess of rivers and springs she had much in common in Tlaloc, and soon they were married. The gods set about recreating all the elements of the world, including humans, out of the ashes of the previous one. Yet again, they required a god to become the sun. This time they asked Chalchiuhtlicue over Tlaloc's protests. Chalchiuhtlicue felt honored by the faith the gods showed in her abilities, and was determined to do her best for the

One day Quetzalcoatl lost his temper, and threw his stone club at his brother in the sky.

fourth world. She climbed into the sky and turned her loving heart upon the fresh, vulnerable creation beneath her. Everything responded joyously to her kindness. The world thrived, plants grew, animals abounded, and people multiplied and learned under her thoughtful reign.

This positive result gnawed at Tezcatlipoca's heart. He did not like to see one succeed where he had failed. He began gossiping about Chalchiuhtlicue to the other gods, and told everyone who would listen that Chalchiuhtlicue was not caring, but calculating. He claimed she manipulated people and gods to make them adore her for her own benefit. "She acts for her own selfish interests and yet everyone praises her," he said to those who would listen.

Despite her remote position far up in the sky, Chalchiuhtlicue heard Tezcatlipoca's words, which was as he intended. The accusation was a terrible blow to the sweet-natured Chalchiuhtlicue and she began to weep. The stress of keeping the world in good order, combined with Tezcatlipoca's insults wore away at her. She could not stop crying.

Chalchiuhtlicue's tears became a terrible deluge that went on for years. It covered the earth, drowned the animals, and offered no place for the birds to land. Eventually, the flood rose so high that the remaining people were forced to climb the highest mountain peaks. Ultimately, the men, women, and children transformed into fish, and leaped into the waves to escape.

The fourth world was at an end. Chalchiuhtlicue departed her position, and the waters began to recede.

These failures cast a gloom upon Quetzalcoatl's thoughts—the gods did not seem capable of creating a harmonious world. For a period of time he was furious at Tezcatlipoca, blaming him for all the ills that had been visited upon the gods' creations. Yet, in his more honest moments he also remembered holding the stone club in his hand, and the jealousy in his heart when he flung it at his brother in the heavens.

Quetzalcoatl decided he would recreate the humans in this fifth world, and he would make them the best version so far. He pondered how he could do this, and remembered that many of the previous generations of humans had died and descended to Mictlán. Quetzalcoatl decided he would go into the underworld and retrieve the bones of dead humans, and use them to revive the human race. His only obstacle would be King Mictlantecuhtli and Queen Mictlancihuatl who fiercely guarded their realm.

Quetzalcoatl went to the god Xolotl for advice, for Xolotl often guided the revered dead to the entrance of Mictlán, and he was familiar with the underworld. He was happy to aid his brother and have an adventure, so the two gods descended into the underworld. They crossed the boundary river, climbed the clashing mountains and the obsidian mountains, walked through the place

of flapping flags, and dodged arrows shot to stop them. They leaped over the ferocious beasts that tried to tear them apart, and slipped through the narrow passage between the hard rocks to come to the great darkness of peace, and the windowless house of Mictlantecuhtli and Mictlancihuatl.

The King and Queen of the Underworld were flattered the gods had taken such great effort to visit them, and their conversation went well. Quetzalcoatl and Xolotl tried not to be unnerved by the skeletal gods, whose piercing eyes seemed incongruous in their fleshless skulls. When all the courtesies were over, Quetzalcoatl made his request respectfully, and The King and Queen granted it. They knew that to retain their position and power, Mictlán needed a constant supply of humans. Quetzalcoatl and Xolotl gathered up human bones and dust from the floor of Mictlán, and began their journey back to the land of the living. Yet, Mictlantecuhtli had a strange sense of humor, and when he bid farewell to Quetzalcoatl, he deliberately jostled the burdened god so that he tripped and dropped his bones. They shattered and broke into many pieces. He gathered them up again, fuming, while Mictlantecuhtli chuckled.

After a long journey, Quetzalcoatl and Xolotl returned to the living world. Quetzalcoatl performed a great rite in which he mixed his own blood with the bones of the deceased, and summoned a new incarnation of the human race. Yet, because of Quetzalcoatl's fall and the breaking of the bones, the people who came into being were a variety of sizes: from tall to very small.

And still, the problem of the fifth sun for the fifth world vexed the gods. They argued the matter in their council, and decided that the position must become permanent—no longer could a god or goddess leave on a whim. At this point they began discussing possible candidates to see if any would be willing to assume the responsibility. Nanahuatl, a poor and afflicted god, was a popular choice because he was humble and hard-working, but to everyone's surprise, wealthy and proud Tecciztecatl also stepped forward.

The gods built a massive bonfire and gathered around it. Tecciztecatl and Nanahuatl were informed that to ascend and transform forever into the sun, they would have to immolate themselves by jumping into the fire. Tecciztecatl stepped forward and ran toward the fire, but at the last moment, its tremendous heat and his fear overcame him. He threw his arms over his face and backed away. Nanahuatl closed his eyes and raced into the fire. He was consumed instantly, and appeared above them in the sky as the blazing sun. The gods cheered and applauded

at the onset of his light. Tecciztecatl, embarrassed and ashamed at his fear, closed his eyes and flung himself into the flames, too.

Another sun appeared in the sky, and the gods gasped. They realized that the earth could not withstand two suns. Quetzalcoatl decided he would not allow the world to fail again. He looked around and spotted a brace of rabbits waiting to be prepared for their celebration feast. He picked one up and threw it with all his strength at the Tecciztecatl sun. It hit the new sun so hard that it dimmed its light forever. From that point onward Tecciztecatl became the moon in the sky, whose pale light waxes and wanes.

The gods and goddesses sat down to their festive meal together and set aside their differences on that new day. They raised their cups and toasted the bright beginning of the world under the light of its fifth sun.

Sekhmet's Thirst

After the world and its people were forged, the great god Ra—he who drives the sun through the sky in the day, and watches over its journey through the underworld at night—observed the progress of his flourishing creation. One of the jewels of human achievement was Heliopolis in Egypt, the city of the sun. Ra was so pleased by its temples, busy streets, and bustling population that he decided to take the form of man and live among his people. Ra became the second Pharaoh of Heliopolis, and under his wise governance, the city was admired throughout the world as a center for culture and peace.

For hundreds of years, Ra ruled justly, and he witnessed the spread of humanity across the earth. However, as the centuries passed, and memories of their origins faded, the people grew haughty, arrogant, and often cruel. Ra watched this with concern, for it appeared they had abandoned *ma'at*: the order that preserved life.

Despite his divinity, as a man Ra suffered the same frailties as mortals. He aged slowly, but over time it became noticeable. Eventually he dyed his hair, his face wrinkled, his hands trembled, and he slept more often. Men and women became bold, snickered about him, and questioned his ability to rule.

"Look at wizened Ra!" they would joke. "His bones are like silver, his flesh like hammered gold, and his hair is the color of lapis lazuli."

Ra's hearing wasn't as sharp as it had been in his prime, but eventually he heard the insults because people stopped whispering their opinions.

When Ra realized that he was the subject of ridicule by the race he had created his wrath burned with intensity like the heat of the midday sun. From his secret mansion in the hidden desert, Ra summoned the gods of Kemet who were in his closest council.

They arrived quietly and carefully so the people of the land would not realize their fate was being weighed on the scales of justice.

Ra sat on his golden throne crowned with a solar disc, and looked at the assembly of Sia, Shu, Heka, Tefnut, Geb,

Nut, and Nun. His fury had not abated, so his voice shook with anger when he asked them how he should proceed.

They said to him, "Call forth your daughter, the apple of your eye, and charge her with your vengeance."

Ra nodded, and in an instant his daughter Hathor appeared and kneeled before him. She laid down her ankh, the key of life. Then Ra channeled the flame of the sun, the Eye of Ra—merciless vengeance—and it engulfed Hathor. She stood, the flames flickered around her, and she became Sekhmet: robed in red, with the head of a lioness, sharp claws on her hands, and eyes blazing with hunger.

Ra marveled at her and said, "Go into the world, Sekhmet, Eye of Ra, and embody my wrath. Destroy the rebellious humans. Make them regret their insolence and heresy."

Sekhmet's response was the thunderous roar of the lioness, eager to hunt. She bounded into *Ta-Mery* with savage abandon.

She strode among the people, an avatar of death, and no one escaped her claws or her teeth. She tore hearts from chests, ripped heads from bodies, and eviscerated stomachs. She drank their blood, and roared with joy at its taste. Weapons made no impact on her. She batted them away and shredded their wielders. Every fight, every death, enflamed her desire for more destruction.

She spared no one. The screams of men, women, and children became a terrifying din that echoed throughout

the world, warning all of the terrible approach of the Eye of Ra.

Sekhmet did not stop after she emptied the first town. She left buildings coated in gore and vital fluids, and continued her merciless rampage. Her fur was matted with blood, and her mouth and arms dripped scarlet.

She had an unceasing appetite.

As Sekhmet continued with her dreadful mission, the gods became increasingly affected by the cries of the doomed. Even Ra's heart softened as pity overcame his anger. In Sekhmet's wake, the rivers ran red.

Finally, Ra called out to Sekhmet: "Daughter, have mercy and cease your butchery. Soon all the people of the world will vanish. I have had enough death to satisfy my anger."

Sekhmet grinned, her fangs streaked red, and laughed. "Father, I am not tired of this sport. My thirst has not been sated. I am vengeance, and every life taken feeds my need for another. I will not stop."

Ra, affronted by Sekhmet's disobedience, raised his voice. "You are the Eye of *Ra!* I command you to cease *now*."

Sekhmet crunched on a thigh bone, and growled. "You set me on the world, and after that you have no control over my actions."

Her roar shook the earth like an earthquake, and she hastened to another village, which was on the road to Heliopolis, where her father had been mocked.

Ra listened to the screams of the anguished, and

> Her fur was matted with blood, and her mouth and arms dripped scarlet.

realized he would need to resort to trickery to end his daughter's bloodlust.

He summoned his messengers, who were swift like the storm winds, and sent them to the island Elephantine, in the river Nile. A fruit grew there that induced sleep, and its juice was the color of blood. Ra's faithful servants returned quickly with baskets of the fruit.

Then he sent word to the brewers in Heliopolis, who quickly began crushing barley, and brewing beer, while others toiled to crush the fruit for its crimson juice. All the time they hammered, pounded, and poured they could hear the battle cries of Sekhmet as she neared the city. Each time her ravenous roars split the air, they redoubled their efforts. The juice was poured into the beer, and three thousand huge clay jars were laid out in front of the main gate.

When blood-soaked Sehkmet approached the city, she noticed what looked like jars of blood. She growled her approval, and bellowed, "Do not think this offering will sway me. I can swallow all of this and still drink your veins dry."

Sekhmet began swigging jar after jar of beer and smacked her lips at the taste. After one thousand jars lay empty, she showed no effect but by the second thousand her voice slurred and she staggered on her feet. By the time she drank another five hundred jars she was sitting, and soon thereafter, powerful Sekhmet fell asleep.

Ra and his retinue arrived, brought her to his mansion, washed the blood from her body, and watched over her.

During Sekhmet's slumber, as sleep cured her fury, she changed and became Hathor again. Several days later Hathor woke and recaptured her ankh.

Before she left she asked Ra, "Was your pride worth this destruction?"

He had no reply.

Hathor then traveled through Egypt, healing and caring for the people.

Heliopolis celebrated its survival, but the world had been gravely hurt, and it took a long time for it to recover.

From that time onward, the Pharaohs of Egypt venerated Sekhmet, and built great statues of her in their cities. Once a year the people drank beer tinged red to commemorate how they survived Sekhmet's thirst.

For she is the merciless fury that once invoked great costs to placate.

Odin's Sacrifice

In Asgard, Land of the Gods of the north, there was no god as shrewd or as clever as Odin, also known as the Allfather. He sat upon his high seat Hlidskjalf, and spied upon everything in the nine worlds, while holding his spear Gungnir, and garbed in his winged helmet and impenetrable armor. There was little he could not do. Every evening the huge ravens Huginn and Muninn alighted upon his shoulders and whispered to him of all that occurred in the world of men. By his feet lay the hulking wolves Geri and Freki. None could approach Odin without them noticing, and no prey escaped their snapping jaws. His glorious wife, Frigg, strong and loyal, was his dear companion and the only one allowed to sit upon the tall throne in his absence.

Yet, at times Odin became restless. With all of his advantages it was hard for him to test himself or rise to a new challenge. Odin's understanding and knowledge were vast, but he sensed there were secrets he could not yet penetrate, and this gnawed at him. He was not a god who was satisfied with ease and safety; his mind was always turning and striving for more.

Odin knew one course he could take that would reveal the unknown to him, but he hesitated. The price was costly, and for a long time he weighed the gain in understanding against the required sacrifice.

On the axis of the nine worlds stood an immense ash tree, Yggdrasil, which sheltered and connected all creation. It had three massive roots, dug deep into different worlds. One root was anchored in Niflheim beside the source of the spring Hvergelmir. Below that, the dragon Nidhogg seethed and devoured corpses and chewed upon the essence of Yggdrasil, trying to unbalance it and overturn creation.

A second root curved into Asgard, and from there bubbled the spring of destiny, attended by the three Norns. They were named Urðr, Verðandi and Skuld: one of them a maid, another a matron, and the last a crone. They determined the lifespan of all beings—including the gods—and Odin had looked upon their faces and trembled at what they knew but withheld. They also poured water from their spring onto Yggdrasil daily, to heal it from the damage wrought by the serpent Nidhogg.

The final root burrowed into Jotunheim, the realm of the giants, who hated the gods. Mimir the Wise was the custodian of the spring, and its Well of Wisdom. Every day he drank from it using the drinking horn, Gjallarhorn, and its waters granted him knowledge of all things. Odin dearly wanted to taste those waters, but Mimir would not hand him the horn for free.

At last Odin made his decision. He grabbed Gungnir, vaulted upon his eight-legged horse Sleipnir, and galloped to Mimir's well before his resolve wavered.

The giant saluted him. "Odin, mighty King," said Mimir, "How may I help you on this fine day?"

Odin leaped from his horse, and stood before the giant. "Give me a drink of water from your well, wise Mimir."

Mimir folded his arms and looked down at Odin sternly. "You know the fee? Everyone must pay it, peasant or nobleman, but none have dared so far."

Odin drew his knife, and gripped the blade tight to still his hand from trembling. "I will be the first."

Odin reached up and gouged out his right eyeball from its socket, and severed its nerve with his knife. The agony caused Odin to fall to his knees, but he did not faint or call out. Mimir took the eye from Odin's bloodied hand, and nodded in respect at the Asgardian.

Then Mimir dunked Gjallarhorn deep into the well's cool waters, and offered the drink to Odin. The king drank deeply, and as he did, future events became clear to him. He witnessed the grief and devastation that would consume humans and gods, and the reasons for them. He also saw the great good that would arise from those conflicts. The knowledge was so vast that Odin's shoulders slumped under its magnitude.

Mimir dropped Odin's eye into the Well of Wisdom, and it sank to the bottom. Forevermore it gleamed up from those clear waters, a sign to all that the Allfather had paid for his wisdom.

After a time Odin composed himself, and the new information settled in his mind. He bound his bleeding eye socket, no longer aware of any pain because his thoughts sparked and spun with delight at the new knowledge. Elated, he comprehended another route to power that would aid both gods and people.

This time he did not hesitate.

He seized a rope, and climbed the trunk of noble Yggdrasil with his spear in his hand. He sat upon one of its branches, and tied one end of the rope to Yggdrasil and the other to his foot. He stripped off his clothes, and looked below at the spring of insight. There was no fear, only certainty.

Odin gripped his spear and threw himself from the ash tree, screaming with joy.

Odin's Sacrifice

The spear pierced his chest, and Odin, greatest of the gods, swung wildly, upside down, bleeding into the waters below.

For nine days and nine nights Odin hung from Yggdrasil, a willing sacrifice to himself and none other.

His wound did not heal, but the drip of blood into the water slowed. And Odin, focused and ecstatic, observed the shapes and forms his blood made as it splashed into and merged with the water.

On the dawn of the tenth day, Odin perceived the mysteries of the universe, how all beings fit into it, and how to bend its fabric to his will.

Roaring, he snapped the rope and fell to the grassy bank of the spring. The sun gleamed across the water, and Odin distinguished the runes of power in its bloody depths.

He plunged his arms into the spring, and scooped out the runes, now solid forms, with his hands.

Instantly he knew how to use them to cure illnesses, to break a weapon in combat, or to crack open fetters. Odin laughed with pleasure as the many purposes of the runes unfurled in his mind. With the right combination he could raise a storm or calm it, start a fire or extinguish it, or

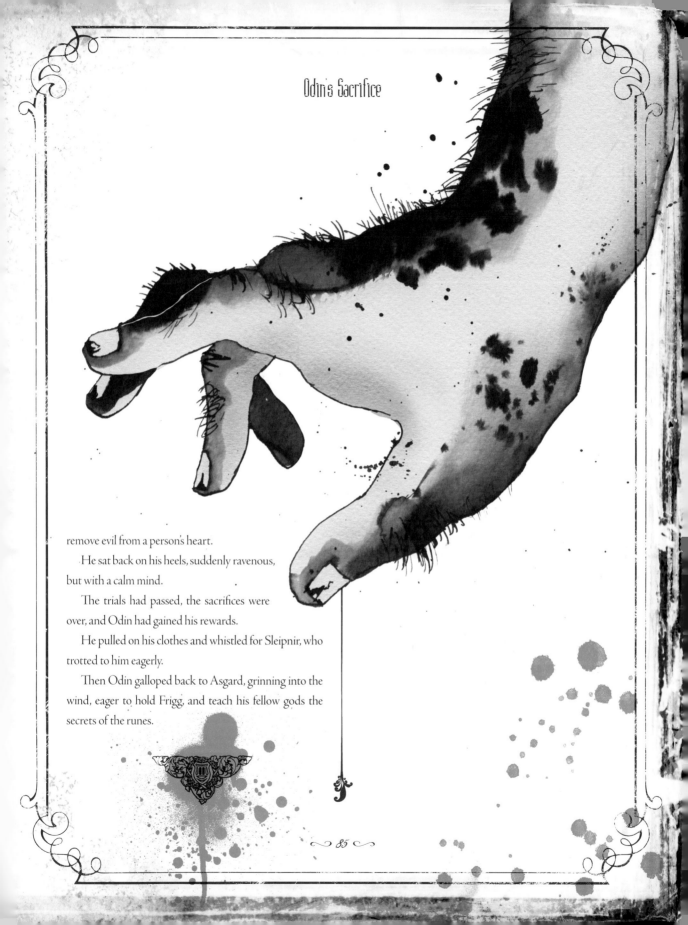

remove evil from a person's heart.

He sat back on his heels, suddenly ravenous, but with a calm mind.

The trials had passed, the sacrifices were over, and Odin had gained his rewards.

He pulled on his clothes and whistled for Sleipnir, who trotted to him eagerly.

Then Odin galloped back to Asgard, grinning into the wind, eager to hold Frigg, and teach his fellow gods the secrets of the runes.

Pele Comes to Hawai'i

Long ago in the great ocean, there floated a magical island called Kuaihelani, which moved about on the whim of the currents. It was rarely sighted by sailors, but when it was, it seemed like a vision of paradise: lush vegetation, banana trees, fine white beaches, and the faint scent of hibiscus. Just as the vision shimmered above the bright blue water, and ships turned toward it, the image would blur and disappear into a haze above the waves. It was a legendary land, and upon it lived legendary people.

One of the couples living on Kuaihelani was Haumea and Moemoe, and they had fourteen children. Many of their children roamed around the island and became engrossed by different aspects of island life. Their oldest daughter, Nāmaka, loved the ocean: its whim and tempers, its storms and peace. If she wasn't swimming like a dolphin in the clear waters around the island, she was on her own traveling over the waves in a canoe, exploring nearby places. Her family joked that her veins ran with salt water, not blood.

Her brother, Kamohoali'i, also swam daily, but he preferred the company of sharks, not men. It was said he could transform into any fish in the ocean, and sometimes he took pity upon those lost at sea and guided them to safe harbors. His brother, Kāne-milo-hai, loved the rich earth, the bright flowers, and the bounty of the land. He was friend to the colorful birds that sang and the little black pigs that darted through the undergrowth. Their other brother, Kane-apua, was fascinated by the wind that churned the sea, and whooshed through the ferns and trees. If he was angry, tempests whipped up, but on an unbearably hot day he was well liked for providing cooling breezes.

They loved their island and the vast ocean that surrounded it, but it was Pele, their sister, who was the most focused and restless of them all. From a young age she sat by her mother's fireplace, staring at the flames, fascinated by their flickering life. At first, Haumea was worried for her daughter, but Pele never got burned. She could pick an orange ember from the center of the fire and hold it in her hand as if it were a cool rock. In fact, the touch of fire made her laugh, but the hearth would explode with sparks if she was in a bad mood. It was often exhausting for Haumea and Moemoe to be parents to such talented children, for their moods and tempers could affect more than just a room.

Their servant, and firekeeper of the hearth, was Lono-makua. He was Pele's best friend. She sat by him and watched how he coaxed a fire back into life from hot coals, and how he banked it down in the evening. As she grew older and graduated from her fire apprenticeship, she sometimes reached out to other sources of fire that simmered under the earth.

Pele and Nāmaka never got along. Fire and water do not mix, and Nāmaka did not approve of her sister's obsession with fire. She only saw its destructive capability,

yet could easily forgive the cruelty of the ocean. Nāmaka watched her younger sister closely, and picked upon her every fault. She berated her mother for being too lenient with Pele, but Haumea had many other children to watch. This is why her last child was born inside an egg. Haumea entrusted Pele to keep the egg warm, which was another point of contention for, her oldest daughter. In a huff at what she believed to be her mother's misplaced trust in Pele, Nāmaka went to her best friend, the ocean, and sailed away to cool her head.

Without her sister's critical attention, Pele finally decided to experiment with her ability to manipulate the molten layer that sizzled under rock.

It was not successful. The island heaved, rock buckled, and jets of lava shot into the air. Pele screamed in both fear and ecstasy. A stream of lava cut across the island and

crawled to the beach. When it met the sea it steamed and hissed, slowed, and then cooled. Nāmaka would know about the accident now—the ocean would tell her.

Haumea and Moemoe had realized for some time that their children would have to leave their homeland. They were too many, and several of them clashed with each other. They looked at the black scar that the lava had left on their island and knew the time had come. Pele had to leave before Nāmaka returned. There would be no island left if they went to war.

Moemoe readied his large canoe called Honuaiakea, which had sails made from fine matting. Kamohoali'i, Kāne-milo-hai, and Kane-apua agreed to go with their sister. Kāne-milo-hai could not look upon the destruction of the island, and wished to see different lands. Kamohoali'i and Kane-apua wanted adventure, and neither of them liked being around when Nāmaka returned. They stocked the canoe with water and food, and at the last moment, as Moemoe and their other siblings pushed them into the water, Haumea handed Pele the egg. Pele tucked the egg into her armpit to keep it warm, and the brothers and sister waved farewell to their family as the canoe crested the waves and headed north to uncharted lands.

They made good time, for the winds blew in their favor, and fresh fish was easy to catch, even without the help of Kamohoali'i. Sometimes he took the form of a massive white shark, and swam beside their canoe. During their voyage the egg cracked, and their little sister Hi'iaka was born. She was well-formed and grew quickly. Within days she walked, swam, and spoke.

Their first stop was a small strip of land they named Moku-papapa, not truly inhabitable, but a fine look-out point. Kāne-milo-hai agreed to stay there to begin making some shelter until the group returned for him later. He waved as they departed, glad to be on firm land again.

They next stopped at a rocky island they named Ni'ihau, which sits high above the ocean. Here, Pele used Pa'oa, her magic stick, as a divining rod, but the result was not auspicious. This was not the place for them to settle. Kane-apua, clumsy in boats, loaded the bow of their canoe and it dipped below the waves. In a rage, Kamohoali'i threw him out of the boat, and they sailed away while Kane-apua pleaded from the shore. Pele said nothing, knowing it was not yet the time to ask forgiveness for Kane-apua. It had been a long trip, and they were all on each other's nerves.

They sailed to the nearby crescent-shaped island they called Lehua, because of the Lehua trees that grew in great abundance upon it. Pele required no divining rod to know it would not serve their purposes. Still, Hi'iaka created a garland of the lehua's fiery red flowers, and placed it upon the ground as a celebration. As they were in a more upbeat mood, Pele spoke tenderly of Kane-apua to Kamohoali'i, and he relented. They swung their canoe

> Sometimes
> he took the form
> of a massive white
> shark, and swam beside
> their canoe.

past Ni'ihau and rescued their marooned brother.

The next island, which they named Kaua'i, seemed perfect. They walked up the mountain, and consulted the Pa'oa near the top. Once again the omens were not good. Frustrated, Pele regarded the lovely island and wished it was otherwise. She decided to continue to trust the rod, and they left the island and climbed back into their canoe. They called the following island O'ahu and the group was optimistic. They walked all over the island for many days, testing the Pa'oa several times, but it always indicated that this was not their new home.

They aimed the boat at the island they named Maui, and its adjunct islets Molokai and Lanai. They searched the little islands quickly, but neither of them fulfilled their needs. On Maui, Pele trekked alone up the massive volcano Haleakalā, feeling the stirring of fire beneath each step. She was sure this was her new home, but the Pa'oa was ambivalent. She sank to the ground, doubting herself. She dug her fingers into the black soil, soothed by the rumblings of the great fire beneath her.

At this point, Nāmaka sailed past Moku-papapa, the first island they had passed, in a fast canoe on a surging wave, rage burning in her soul. She had trailed her brothers and sister with the icy determination of a sea wolf. Beside her swam a sea dragon named Huai. Kāne-milo-hai spotted his sister and her ominous companion and called out to her. "Nāmaka, where are you going so fast?"

Pele summoned her fire and blasted Nāmaka who screamed in agony.

As she sped by, she yelled, "To destroy Pele, the most irresponsible of sisters." The memory of the scarring of her homeland, Kuaihelani, arose in her mind, along with her resentment at how her parents had covered once again for the spoiled brat. She clenched her teeth and aimed straight for Maui, where she would find her foe.

Just before the beach, Nāmaka dove into the water and her fury fueled her transformation into a sea dragon.

Together the two dragons lifted their heads and howled for Pele's blood.

Pele heard the challenge, and knew she could not escape her sister. She lifted her chin, and marched down to the beach, where the water churned from the sea dragons' bodies.

There was no pause for speeches or pleas. At the sight of Pele, Nāmaka roared and dove at her sister. Pele summoned her fire and blasted Nāmaka who screamed in agony. But, Haui flanked Pele and caught her in his mouth. He broke her bones before he threw her limp body at Nāmaka.

Nāmaka bellowed in triumph. She snapped Pele in two with her vicious teeth, and dismembered her further with her claws. Then Nāmaka tossed the remains of her sister on Kahikinui, where her bones form a hill to this day. Exultant, Nāmaka returned to her human form and sailed away with Haui.

Kamohoali'i, Kane-apua, and Hi'iaka rushed to the beach too late to save Pele. Her blood was spattered and smeared over the sand. They shed tears of anguish and anger, but then Hi'iaka looked across the Alenuihāhā channel at the island of Hawai'i, which they had yet to visit.

The volcanoes Mauna-loa and Mauna-kea erupted into flame, and black smoke plumed upward. In the smoke, the spirit-form of Pele danced, rapturous at her transformation and homecoming. Her brothers and sister dried their eyes and smiled, for their sister had become the Goddess of Fire, and wedded forever to the islands of Hawai'i.

As Nāmaka returned past Moku-papapa she reported her victory to Kāne-milo-hai. He grinned, and pointed to the fire and billowing smoke from the island of Hawai'i, in which Pele's form was clearly visible.

Nāmaka screamed in fury, and began turning her canoe back to continue her conflict.

Kane-milo-hai felt pity for his obsessed sister. "Nāmaka, you cannot win now," he said. "Pele has become a spirit. She is invincible."

Nāmaka glared at Hawai'i a final time, and turned away from her defeat.

The Magician's Head

In times past, the ancestor god Odùduwà created a great kingdom called Yorubaland, which nestled in the crook of Africa. All the kings of the Yoruba people traced their lineage to Odùduwà, and they felt obliged to live up to his conquering spirit.

His grandson, Oranyan, was a warrior prince with 150 seasoned fighters as his personal guard. He founded the city Oya, which became the center of the Oya Empire. He was the first descendent of Odùduwà to be both Oba (king) and Alaafin (emperor). His eldest son, Ajaka, succeeded on Oranyan's death, but Ajaka possessed none of his father's restless need for dominion. Ajaka was peaceful and uninterested in expanding the empire. The minor Obas in the region noticed, and they encroached upon his territory. The Yoruba people, unhappy at fending off attacks while their king did nothing, removed Ajaka from the throne. His younger brother, Sango, was named Alaafin instead.

Ajaka was exiled to Igbodo. Banished from his friends and family, alone among strangers and no longer respected, Ajaka's demeanor changed. For seven bitter years he lived in Idbodo, waiting for a chance to prove himself anew.

Sango made up for his brother's mild disposition, for he was wild and hot-tempered. It was said he could blow fire and smoke from his mouth, which frightened his enemies. He welcomed war like an old friend. Throughout his reign, Sango battled all those who opposed him, and secured his empire. He was also fond of making spells, and discovered the secret of conjuring lightning.

One day he traveled to the top of the hill above Oya with his retinue of friends and warriors, to put his spell to the test. He raised his arms, and called to the heavens. Accordingly, a storm boiled up, and smoky, orange clouds settled over Oya. Alarmed, Sango started to move down the hill to his city, but it was too late.

Sizzling bolts of lightning slammed into Oya's buildings. Thunder boomed, knocking Sango and his entourage to their feet, and deafened them. Fires erupted across the high arches of the thatched houses. The people

trapped inside screamed in terror and pain as the flames roared through the rooms, whipped up by the sudden winds.

The people worked all night to extinguish the flames, and in the morning, when the tempest faded away, they began to reckon their losses. Coated in soot, Sango discovered that many of his wives and children had perished. Crazed by grief, he decided to abdicate his throne for bringing such misfortune upon his family and his people. When his courtiers tried to dissuade him, Sango grabbed his sword and threatened to kill them if they did not let him go.

Sango and a few followers departed the smoking city to the sound of the wails of the mourners. Over time, even Sango's most dedicated servants abandoned him when he would not listen to reason. Alone, and overcome with remorse, Sango hanged himself. Thereafter, his people considered him the god of thunder and lightning, and whenever lightning flashed and thunder rolled, they would call out his name and salute him.

Thus, Ajaka returned from exile and was restored as Alaafin in Oya. He began his reign by waging war on all the Obas who had dismissed him in the past, and those he suspected of treason. He engaged experts in magic, and they cast spells against his enemies. Before he entered the field of battle, he sent before him flocks of huge, brightly colored birds armed with arrows. They flew over the enemy and showered arrows upon them—thinning their numbers and scattering them. His follow-up attack decimated his foes. Ajaka exhibited neither sympathy nor mercy for those he conquered. He kept the skulls of all the Obas he slaughtered, and soon there was a huge white mound of them in a shrine in Oya. Often, Ajaka would go into the room, lit by candles, and stare at the hundreds of empty eye sockets of those he had slain.

Then he would sit upon his elephant-tusk throne, dressed in finely embroidered robes, lion skin, and gold jewelry, satisfied that none would dare oppose him.

At this time, Ajaka's three best magicians requested an audience in his throne room, and asked if they could return to their homes. With no more battles to fight, Paku, Teteoniru, and Elenre were bored. They wished to be free of Ajaka, and shake off the dust of Oya and its anxious people.

Ajaka glared down at them from his seat. In his mind every request was a concealed betrayal. Ajaka imagined what harm these men could do if they took refuge with one of his enemies. After all, he had trained them well in the use of magic for war.

Ajaka said, "You do not have my permission to leave! You are my servants. I tell *you* when you are dismissed."

The faces of the three men hardened, for magicians do not take well to intimidation.

The people worked all night to extinguish the flames, and in the morning, when the tempest faded away, they began to reckon their losses.

The Magician's Head

Paku stepped forward, "Alaafin, we asked politely as a courtesy, but do not think you can restrain us against our will."

Ajaka, unused to disobedience, reddened and roared, "You will do as I say!"

Paku grinned, and bowed with a great flourish. Then he hopped into the air and vanished.

Ajaka lunged to his feet, and stared at Teteoniru and Elenre. His servants backed away.

Then, Teteoniru also bowed, and removed a ball of twine from his robe. He threw the string into the air, and it hung fast like a pole. Teteoniru climbed up nimbly and also disappeared.

Ajaka, his cheeks puffing in fury, stared at Elenre. "You better vanish like your companions, Elenre, or you will suffer!"

Elenre straightened his shoulders, and with a calm voice said, "You cannot harm me."

Incensed, Ajaka pointed at his best warrior, and bellowed "Cut off his arrogant head!"

The guard flexed his huge muscles and drew his sword. Elenre remained still with a serene expression. The soldier aimed a terrible blow at Elenre's neck, but the sword shattered, and the warrior screamed—his right arm had withered.

Ajaka yelled over the cries, and pointed at his spearmen. "Drive your spears into his belly!" Despite their trepidation several men did as their king commanded, but the spears disintegrated when they touched Elenre's skin.

Ajaka ordered Elenre be dragged out of the palace and thrown on the ground of the compound. Elenre did not resist, and lay in the dust peacefully. Twenty of the royal guards hauled a massive boulder over to the spot and dropped it on Elenre. But it seemed as light as a ball of cotton to Elenre, who batted it away easily. He sat up in a comfortable position under the blazing sun.

Ajaka reined in his temper. He left Elenre guarded by a ring of soldiers and returned to his throne. He summoned a messenger and told him to fetch Elenre's wife, Ijaehin. A short while later, the messenger returned, dragging Ijaehin. She prostrated herself before the King.

Ajaka stared down at her trembling body. "Your husband has insulted me gravely. Tell me how I may harm him, and you shall have a favored spot in my household." He waved to his guards and they lowered their weapons. "Otherwise it will be your blood spilled today."

After a few slaps and some more coaxing, Ijaehin revealed her husband's weakness. "Pull a blade of grass from the thatch of our house. With that alone you can decapitate him."

Ajaka issued the command, and walked outside to witness the deed. He ordered Ijaehin to watch Elenre's execution, so the magician would realize who betrayed him.

The blade of grass hummed through the air, and Elenre's head flew off his shoulders. It bounced several times and smacked against Ajaka's right hand.

Ajaka howled in fear, and shook his hand, weighed down by Elenre's head, but it would not fall off. His strongest servants attempted to yank the head off but the more they pulled the more Ajaka screamed in pain.

Elenre's head became Ajaka's permanent companion. It spoke to him constantly, making fun of him, and undermining his rule when he sat on his throne and gave orders as emperor. Ajaka couldn't sleep, or eat, for whenever he tried to use his right hand during meals the head would lunge at the food and eat it first.

Ajaka summoned all the magicians in the kingdom to help him remove Elenre's head, but many would not attend because of Elenre's reputation. A myriad of spellcasters and enchanters tried rituals and spells, but nothing worked. Elenre's derisive laughter followed them out of the palace when they failed.

Ajaka began to waste away and became morose. None of his wives would visit him because of the disgusting things Elenre said to them. Nothing he tried, such as sewing up Elenre's lips, worked. Needles and knives blunted on his flesh, and no other grass blade did him any harm.

Months later, Ajaka was slouched on his throne. His clothing engulfed his emaciated body, and his eyes were closed against the tirade of insults from Elenre. An elderly

magician called Agawo entered the room, and Elenre yelled at him, "Do you think you can affect me?"

The man fell down on the ground before the throne, and cried, "Who am I to oppose you noble Elenre? I am no better than my predecessors whom you have already defeated. I came in obedience to the king's commands, for I dare not refuse his call."

At that, Elenre let out a long sigh. "I salute your wisdom Agawo, and your bravery despite your knowledge of my ability. I yield to your humility," and Elenre glared one final time at Ajaka, "a trait missing in many."

With that, his head detached from Ajaka, and rolled out of the palace. At its final resting spot a river sprang up

called Odo Elenre.

Akaja often dreamed of Elenre at night. In those nightmares, the head remained stuck to his hand and the crafty magician whispered, "I will be with you always, Akaja. You will *never* escape me."

White Buffalo Woman

One year the spring fires roared across the plains, burning the stale grasses, and stampeding the buffalo, antelope, and deer before its snapping embers. Nothing eased its hunger, and even the seven Lakota nations, used to the cycle of fire, rains, and regrowth, were taken aback by its savage attack and choking smoke. Many died during that terrible burning, but there was little time to mourn as they fled on foot from the fire's appetite. When the fires eased at last, they waited for the nourishing rains that always followed, which would transform the scorched plains into an undulating sea of lush grasses.

Yet, the skies remained flat blue except for the roasting sun, and no clouds gathered. The blistering winds blew dust, and the lakes and pools shrank. The only shade was inside the tepee, or the shadow it cast on the cracked earth. Little could be done during the high heat of the day. The people sat and fanned their children, and gazed up at the pitiless sky, anxious for signs of rain. Animals collapsed, their tongues swollen and protruding, under the suffocating weight of the constant heat. The only creatures that prospered were the vultures. They swooped down on their great black wings and sauntered happily among the corpses and clouds of flies.

Soon, the people's supplies dwindled, and scouting for game to eat became as difficult as divining water. The chiefs of the seven nations decided to combine their resources during this crisis. The elders of the Oceti Sakowin—seven council fires—sat in council together at night, when the temperature was bearable, and traded stories and memories of previous times of famine.

Every morning scouts were sent from each band to search for food, and every evening they returned with little save for a few scrawny prairie dogs. The buffalo vanished. It was as if the earth shunned the Lakota.

Early one morning, Chief Standing Hollow Horn of the Itazipcho, the Without-Bows, chose two of his finest hunters, Little Bear and Jumping Eagle, to search for game. They left the forest of tepees and walked into the scorching, arid plains. They searched everywhere,

White Buffalo Woman

but found no trace of any animal except ragged vultures that roosted far up in dead trees. They sighted a hill, and agreed to climb it so they could have a commanding view of the plains.

Sweating and exhausted, they had to stop for a short rest when they were still on the foot of the hill. Breathing hard, they squatted in the shadow of an outcrop. Heat rose from the shriveled land, and in its haze they noticed a blurred, bright shape approaching them. Soon they realized it was a figure, but it glided across the earth as if floating. Jumping Eagle hopped up on a rock to get a better vantage point, and shaded his eyes against the glare.

Little Bear remained low, and glanced up at his friend. "That stranger must be *wakan*," he said, "only a holy person could move so freely in this furnace."

As the shape moved closer it snapped into focus, and they realized it was the fairest woman they had ever seen. She was dressed in gleaming white buckskin, embroidered with colorful porcupine quills in sacred designs. Dots of red face paint adorned her cheeks, and her glossy black hair hung loose except for a band of buffalo fur across her forehead keeping it in place. Her dark eyes sparkled with insight and power. In her hands, she carried a large bundle wrapped in white bison skin, and a fan of sage leaves.

Both of them stared at her, entranced at this vision of mystery.

Jumping Eagle whispered to his friend, "What a wonder, and she is all alone. I could steal her away and make her my wife."

Little Bear glared at his friend. "That would be sacrilege! Don't—"

But Jumping Eagle stepped off his perch, and walked boldly toward the woman. His intentions were clear from his swagger and how one hand grasped the horn hilt of his sheathed dagger. The woman's benevolent expression didn't change. He reached out to touch her... and a whirlwind of dust appeared around him instantly. After a few moments, a warm breeze sprang up and dispersed the cloud, leaving the woman visible. By her feet lay a pile of cleaned human bones and a skull. Writhing among the bones were a variety of deadly snakes, hissing and rattling their tails, and their bright black eyes fixed intently on Little Bear.

He dropped to one knee and cast his face downward to show his respect. When he looked up again she smiled at him.

"Fear not, your heart is filled only with good intentions, unlike your wicked friend. My name is *Ptesan Winyan*, White Buffalo Calf Woman, and I carry a message from *Tatanka Oyate*, the buffalo nation, as well as a sacred gift. Return to your camp and tell your chief to prepare for my arrival. Erect a medicine lodge with twenty-four poles, make it holy for my coming, and assemble your people in it."

With this, she walked back into the waves of heat rising from the blanched earth and vanished.

Little Bear's fatigue disappeared and he sprinted back to the encampment. Gasping for breath, he related everything to Chief Standing Hollow Horn. The chief ordered several tepees to be sewn together to construct a medicine lodge as White Buffalo Calf Woman had directed, and their medicine man purified it. They waited for four days, until finally a scout called out that a woman clad in shining white buckskin was walking toward the camp.

All the men, women, and children crowded into the medicine lodge, and Chief Standing Hollow Horn himself guided *Ptesan Winyan* into the huge space. The people hushed when they saw her, and not even the babies cried. She carried the bundle wrapped in white buffalo skin, and walked around the tepee clockwise several times.

When she finished, the chief spoke, and his voice was thick with respect, "Sister, we are honored you have chosen us for your teaching. We cannot offer you any meat, for we have none worthy of your dignity." He dipped sweet grass into a skin bag of water, and said, "All we can offer you is water." The woman took the water gratefully, and instructed the people to create an altar in the middle of the space.

Then she carefully unwrapped her bundle, and revealed a marvelous *chanupa*, a sacred pipe. She held it up so everyone could see it. Its bowl was made from red stone, and carved on it was the image of a buffalo. The

stem was crafted from wood, and from it hung twelve Spotted Eagle feathers.

"This is a precious gift from *Tatanka Oyate*. Only those with a pure spirit should ever touch it."

Then she bowed and showed those present how to properly hold the pipe, how to pray while filling it with red willow-bark tobacco, and its use in ritual. She also explained that the *chanupa* represented the connection between the Lakota and the world.

"When you use the pipe you become a living prayer. You stand upon the earth, our mother. You breathe in the smoke of the tobacco and release it up into the sky. The bowl carved with the buffalo represents our world and our four-legged relatives, the wooden stem is all the plants that grow, and the feathers symbolize the winged creatures. When you connect to the pipe and breathe in the smoke, you become a bridge between the earth, the domain of humans and animals, and the Great Mystery above. You affirm your part in this sacred wheel of life."

She also pointed out seven circles carved into the bowl of the *chanupa*. *Ptesan Winyan* explained they represented the seven ceremonies that the pipe would be used for, and she demonstrated the first rite to those assembled. "Later, you will learn the other six," she promised.

She got up to leave, and paused. "The *chanupa* will show you a red life and a red road. Respect it, and your

He dropped to one knee and cast his face downward to show his respect. When he looked up again she smiled at him.

people will prosper. It will take you to the end of the road. Within me are the four ages of creation. I will look for you in every age, and at the end I will return."

At this, White Buffalo Calf Woman left the medicine lodge and all the tribespeople filed out silently to watch her departure from the camp. Their hearts were suffused with awe, for they realized they had witnessed a turning point for their people. All would be changed forever.

Ptesan Winyan raised her hand and said, *"Toksha ake wacinyanktin ktelo—*I will see you again." Then she walked into the scorching prairie. After a short distance, she turned to regard the people again, and sat down on the dusty earth. When she stood up,

she had transformed into a young black buffalo calf. The calf walked farther away, and then lay down and rolled over. When she arose she had changed into a brown buffalo. The next time she laid down and rolled over, she came to her feet as a red buffalo. The buffalo trotted on until she was a dot on the horizon. At the last moment, she rolled over again, and became a white buffalo calf. The white buffalo bowed to the four directions of the earth, and disappeared.

Moments later the people heard the sound of buffalo's snorting and their hooves upon the earth. Herds of buffalo appeared near the camp. They were peaceful and allowed the Lakota to kill them so

Moments later the people heard the sound of buffalo's snorting and their hooves upon the earth.

the people could survive. In respect of their sacrifice, the Lakota used all of the buffalo and let none of their bodies go to waste, and they offered up prayers and thanks to *Tatanka Oyate* and *Ptesan Winyan* for their gifts.

A cool breeze sprang up, and clouds heavy with water drifted across the sky. That night a heavy rain pounded their tepees, and by the morning it tapered off temporarily to a light mist.

Dawn's light swept across the prairie, conjuring rainbows in the drizzle, and revealing tiny green shoots spearing up from the mud.

Life had returned to the plains, and the Lakota.

The People of Mud, Flesh, and Wood

Before the creatures of the earth existed, before they had land to run upon or plants to eat, there was only one vast ocean, the languid sky, and silence. In that silence, there abided powerful gods. Although they resided in peace, after a time they came together and discussed bringing other beings into existence. Oldest among them was Xmucane and Xpiacoc, mother and father of them all. Then there was the Heart of the Sky, known as Huracan, Gucumatz, the serpent covered with green feathers, and Tepeu the sovereign. Huracan, Gucumatz, and Tepeu conferred together in the quiet gloom, and conceived of a plan to create life.

They spoke the word "Earth," and the ground erupted from the waters, breaking it into smaller oceans and seas. They called for mountains and hills, and they rose up from the land. Rivers, mighty and small, spilled down from these heights across the plains and emptied into the seas. Trees, shrubs, plants, and grass grew immediately, covering the earth with lush, green vegetation. Afterward, the gods summoned animals into existence, so there

were deer leaping through the grasses, and birds soaring through the skies. The puma and the jaguar appeared too, eyes flashing like jewels as they stalked their prey. And below them in the undergrowth were the serpents. Fish dashed through the rivers, and swam into the ocean where the sharks chased them. The world was filled with animal cries and squawks, but none of them could speak with the gods or thank the divine beings for their existence.

Huracan, Gucumatz, and Tepeu turned to Xmucane and Xpiacoc, and they agreed to shape new beings who would be capable of speech.

Xmucane and Xpiacoc first created people whose bodies were fashioned from earth and mud. It did not work well. If they stepped into a stream their legs dissolved, and a deluge of rain melted them down into lumps. If they held anything too heavy it would slide through their hands. Their form had no stability, and they could not multiply. Recognizing their mistake, Xmucane and Xpiacoc toppled their creations and pondered the best way to create a new race.

The People of Mud, Flesh, and Wood

This time they carved effigies from wood that could speak and reproduce. The wooden mannequins looked like people, could speak, and move around the world. They built farms and cities, and they flourished. Yet, they didn't have hearts or minds, blood or sweat, and they didn't know their makers. Their faces were masks, and their limbs rigid. They wandered stiffly through the world with no purpose, terrorized the animals and birds, and abused the forests and the wealth of the earth.

Displeased, Huracan called forth a terrible flood that roared across the lands and smashed many of the wooden people. After the waters subsided, the creatures of the earth and the wooden people's own implements attacked them, in revenge for their mistreatment. The timber people ran away, and climbed upon the roofs of their houses for safety. The buildings refused to support them and tipped them off. Birds swooped down and pecked their eyes out. Jaguars bounded from the forest and tore them apart. The very millstones the people had used to grind maize rose up and rolled over their limbs, breaking and pulverizing them. Their camp fires burst up hot and hungry and set them on fire. Pots and pans pummeled them into a mush. Dogs and turkeys nipped and pecked at what remained, and scattered their remnants about. Huracan spoke a word and black clouds rolled across the skies. Lightning flashed and a thunderous rain poured down, eradicating all trace of the heartless mannequins.

For a time after this, the gods were preoccupied with other events before they once again turned their thoughts to bringing forth a people with whom they could converse and enjoy. After their failed experiments they had a better appreciation of what could work, and what could bring about disaster. Xmucane and Xpiacoc thought long and hard, and using yellow and white maize they formed four perfect men. Their names were Balam Quitzé (Jaguar with the Sweet Smile), Balam Agab (Jaguar of the Night), Mahucutah (The Distinguished Name), and Iqi Balam (Jaguar of the Moon). They had neither a father nor a mother—for they were brought into being by the divine work of Xmucane and Xpiacoc alone.

The gods keenly observed the four men when they woke up for the first time. The men were intelligent, could speak and converse, and could hold and use implements. Because they contained the divine essence of Xmucane and Xpiacoc, they knew everything and understood their origin. Xmucane and Xpiacoc spoke to the four humans and told them to look around at the sky, land, plants, and animals, and acknowledge their part in it. Balam Quitzé, Balam Agab, Mahucutah, and Iqi Balam gave thanks to their creators, calling them Grandmother and Grandfather for giving them form and senses with which to behold the world.

If there was anything wrong with the men, it was that they perceived too much of the world and the gods.

Warned by their past failures, Xmucane and Xpiacoc worried that the men would become prideful and arrogant if there was nothing for them to know or to strive to understand. So, Huracan breathed upon the mens eyes, and a thin veil coated them, reducing their ability to see everything and understand all there was to know of the gods and creation.

When the men slept, Xmucane and Xpiacoc created four perfect women: Cahapaluna (Sky Sea House), Choimha (Shrimp House), Tzununiha (Hummingbird House), and Caquixaha (Macaw House). Huracan breathed upon their eyes too, so they had the same veiled understanding of the world as the men. When the eight men and women woke up together, they marveled at each other's strength and beauty, and soon they paired off into four couples.

Yet, the world was still in darkness, for there was no sun. The people settled and formed communities, had many children, and called themselves the Quiché people, but they lived in a world of gloom. They fasted and called out to their gods, asking for light by which they could sow food and see one another properly for the first time. They received no answer, and the sun did not rise. Finally, all the Quiché people, headed up by the four original couples, set out in pilgrimage for Tulan Zuyva, the citadel of Seven Caves and Seven Canyons, reputed to be the holy domain of the gods. When the people arrived, a god came out and selected

each of the four couples. Thus Balam Quitzé was received by the god Tohil. Balam Agab was acknowledged by the god Avilix, and Mahucutah by the god Hacavitz. Iqi Balam was selected by Nicacah Tacah, but the first three gods were the greatest, and it was in this way that the Quiché people divided into three groups. When they left Tulan Zuyva, the languages of the three groups diverged, and they could no longer understand each other clearly.

At this time the people did not have fire, but the god Tohil knew its secret. He gave them fire, and when they departed Tulan Zuyva they brought it back to their towns and villages. It gave them light in the darkness, kept them warm, and cooked their food. They praised Tohil for this prized gift. One freezing evening, a hard hail hit their towns and extinguished every fire. Balam Quitzé and Balam Agab cried out to Tohil for aid. He appeared, and hunkered down before the two men. He spun a little stick expertly between his hands on a flat piece of wood, with shavings around it. After a moment smoke rose, and the shavings curled up red with flames. Tohil showed them how to layer more leaves and twigs upon the sparks to build a larger fire, and from that moment, the two men knew the secret and they told their brothers and wives.

Although the Quiché people delighted in the fire, they yearned for a star, or the sun, to break through the monotonous dark. Long had it been promised to them

> If there was anything wrong with the men, it was that they perceived too much of the world and the gods.

by the gods, and they worried why it didn't happen. In the end they consulted oracles, and all the nations moved as one to the mountain they called Hacavitz, to wait upon the top, and fast and pray for the sun. They carried the gods Tohil, Avilix, and Hacavitz with them, hung garlands of flowers around them, and burned copal incense in their honor.

After a long while it was the Morning Star that first appeared—initially a tiny dot of light, barely noticeable in the black sky, and then a glittering beauty that heralded hope. The people raised their many voices and different tongues in chants, burned more copal incense in celebration of the star, and what they hoped would follow. Their prayers boomed out from the mountain top, and

echoed in the valleys below, while the smoke rose up into the air as the Morning Star gleamed down on the people.

The sky lightened, blushed pink, and the sun rose into the sky for the first time. All the birds cried in joy at the sight. Parrots, the eagles and white vultures, all the small and great birds, spread their wings and beat them like applause. The people turned their faces toward the sun and wondered at its light and heat. The pumas and the jaguars roared their approval from the jungle, and the other animals celebrated with calls and hoots.

This new sun, burning hot from its birth, instantly dried out the earth, which had long been soggy from when it rose from the water. The people soon shrank under the torment of its heat, and hid under tents as it burned its

path across the blue sky. The three gods of the Quiché, Tohil, Avilix, and Hacavitz turned to stone, along with a puma and jaguar, a rattlesnake and a pit viper, first among the animals. They became a permanent monument to the appearance of the day star. After the sun's first trip across the sky, twilight deepened into black, but it was no longer truly dark. The night sky was festooned with stars and constellations, and then the moon appeared, soft compared to the sun's harsh glare.

The people crept out into the still, cool night air, and stood before the stone gods and animals, under the peaceful light of the stars and moon, and burned incense in their honor. Never would people suffer true darkness again.

The next morning, the sun rose again to the people's cries of joy and happiness. So the sun has risen every morning thereafter, as a reward for the consistency and faith of the original Quiché people. It is said that the sun was fiercer and hotter then, and what the ancestors of the Quiché see today is but a pale mirror of that first sun, which blazed down upon the fresh mountain full of the first people of the world, their faces raised in awe, and arms aloft in praise.

Nu Wa Saves the World

In the great void before creation, nothing existed. This absence attracted energy. At first it appeared as tendrils of smoke, which spun and twisted around itself until it coalesced into an eggshell. Inside the egg the energy split into two complementary forces: Yang, which became pure and light; and Yin, which took on a heavy, murky quality. As they brushed up against each other, a being came into existence named Pan Gu. For eighteen thousand years, Pan Gu slept at the center of the egg while Yang and Yin whispered to him about what was yet to come.

Finally, Pan Gu stirred. He lifted his face for the first time and yawned. Horns sprouted from his forehead, and his body was covered in thick hair. He tried to get up but the tips of his horns tapped against the egg that contained him. He spread his hands and feet and felt the confines of his prison. In the moment it took him to wonder how he could escape, a magical axe appeared in his hand. He swung it at the shell and it cracked, which was the first sound in the universe (other than Pan Gu's snores).

Immediately, Yang and Yin slipped out of the egg, and Pan Gu kicked apart the rest of the shell. Yang began to rise upward, and Yin sank a little. Pan Gu watched the two energies and realized they needed to remain separate. He stood upon Yin, raised his arms, and pushed Yang upward. Yin became the earth, and Yang the sky. Pan Gu remained between them, and he underwent nine changes every day, informed by the wisdom of the sky and the strength of the earth. Pan Gu also grew ten feet taller daily; thus the gap between the sky and the earth increased. In this fashion another eighteen thousand years passed, and Pan Gu become a giant 90,000 li (36,000 miles) tall.

Yet, Pan Gu was tired. He knew the sky and the earth had stabilized, and he realized it was time for a more profound change.

He shouted farewell, and it shook the heavens and the earth. His last word is the thunder that still echoes in the world today. His final breath was a long sigh, and it became all the winds upon the earth—the frightening whirlwinds as well as the refreshing zephyrs. His body disintegrated as he willed himself into the world. His left eye shot out hot and bright into the sky and evolved into the sun. His right eye drifted up, pale and milky, to form the moon. His facial hair spun out to create the stars and the galaxies. Then Pan Gu's body crashed to the earth and made the mountains. His head became Mount Tai in the east, and his upturned feet became Mount Hua in the west. His belly formed Mount Song, while his left arm became Mount Heng in the south, and his right Mount Heng in the north.

Pan Gu's blood splashed over the land and became the first rivers, while his muscles decomposed to create the soil for lush pastures. His sweat fell upon the earth as rain and nourished it. His body hair turned into bushes and forests. Pan Gu's bones and teeth sank into the wet earth and transformed into valuable minerals such as jade, gold, and diamonds. In four locations, where these most precious materials resided, grew the pillars of heaven, which shot up to support the firmament above.

In that final moment, when the last of Pan Gu was sacrificed to create the world, one being sprang up: Nü Wa, the first goddess. The lower half of her body was that of a large, powerful serpent, and her torso was like that of a woman.

For hundreds of years Nü Wa slipped across the world alone. As the inheritor of Pan Gu's power, she spent much of her time cultivating the earth and creating animals and birds to populate it. One of her favorite creations was the giant turtle Ao, who swam in the southern seas. All this work kept her busy, and she learned many arts and skills. She fashioned beautiful clothing for herself, and built a wonderful palace in which to live. Yet, she had no one to converse with or to discuss all she had come to understand. She did not know a word for loneliness, but experienced it deeply in her soul. Nü Wa always felt more at peace by water, so she often sat on the grassy bank by a lake with her tail dipped into the water, and sang a song of sorrow. The cranes standing in the still pool bowed their graceful red-crowned heads in tribute to her pain.

One day Nü Wa slumped as she ended her lament, and noticed the reflection of her sad features in the lake. There is nothing like me in the world, she thought, and at first the pain of that realization was a hammer strike to her heart. Yet, it was quickly followed by another, happier idea. There is no need for me to linger on my own, she thought, and smiled. I shall create people to share the world with me.

At that, Nü Wa straightened up with purpose.

She took a handful of mud and sculpted a person with two arms and two legs. When she was pleased with her efforts, she placed it upon the grass and blew upon it to dry it out. Immediately, the person began to grow in

Nü Wa Saves the World

size, and soon it was an adult. It jumped up and danced, and called Nü Wa mother. Nü Wa clapped with delight, and began creating more people in the same way. Soon there were many people around her, but Nü Wa found the labor exhausting. After two days of constant work, she took a break and noticed her clothes were splattered with mud. She flicked a glob of wet earth off her silk robe. When it landed on the earth it transformed into one of her little people and grew into an adult just like the others.

Nü Wa realized she could make her people much faster now. She spied a vine nearby, and dragged it through the mud. Then she shook it violently and blobs of mud showered the ground around her. From each splatter of mud a person arose. She soon created a large group of people. Her first lesson to them was how to dress in leaves to protect against the weather, and which fruits were safe to consume. Over time she taught them how to build homes and cultivate crops, and she encouraged them to sing and dance to celebrate

the many gifts they had in their beautiful world.

Soon Nü Wa's people formed communities and towns, and spread across the world. She passed her time traveling between them, and talking to all her children. She was content to reside with them upon the earth, guiding their lives.

As the world grew older, and humanity flourished and adapted, gods appeared in the heavens—some of them were people who ascended to divinity because of their selfless deeds during their lives. The most revered among them was the Jade Emperor, who ruled the heavens and established order among the gods, goddesses, and the spirit world. Yet, not everyone in the celestial realm was pleased with this system. Gong Gong, the god of water, who took the form of a huge black dragon, resented his position and believed the errands assigned to him were too menial for his divine power. He plotted with a dreadful spirit named Xiang Yao, who had nine heads and the body of a snake, to overthrow the rule of heaven and cast down the Jade Emperor.

Gong Gong began his assault on heaven and unleashed devastating floods upon the world of humans. Nü Wa frantically tried to help the vulnerable people who were being swept away by the torrential waters, while above, Gong Gong and Xiang Yao battled to usurp the Jade Emperor. They were opposed by the heavily-armored fire god Zhu Rong, who rode upon a tiger and fought with a magical sword. The gods fought

Gong Gong began his assault on heaven and unleashed devastating floods upon the world of humans.

back and forth across the heavens. Gong Gong's ebony talons lashed at Zhu Rong, while the fire god's sword dashed embers as it blocked the ferocious attacks. Even with the aid of Xiang Yao, Gong Gong could not defeat Zhu Rong.

Infuriated, and refusing to accept the shame of defeat, Gong Gong hurled himself from heaven and smashed into Mount Buzhou, which was also the base of one of the pillars of heaven. A huge section of mountain collapsed, the pillar toppled, and it tore a terrible rip in the sky. Awful creatures from beyond poured through this wound in existence and ravaged the planet. Flood and fire roared across the earth. The three remaining pillars of heaven cracked and swayed under the uneven weight of heaven and the devastation on earth. Hundreds of thousands of people drowned, burned, or were shredded by demons, and the horror of it crushed the people's spirit.

The sight of this destruction appalled Nü Wa. Her entire purpose was to nourish life and safeguard Pan Gu's first act of creation. She could not allow it to be undone by the petty spite of Gong Gong. Yet, to save the world she would have to sacrifice one she loved dearly. Weeping, Nü Wa killed the turtle Ao, and cut off his four legs. She replaced the four pillars of heaven with Ao's limbs, and propped the sky back up. Then she gathered five precious stones of different colors from a riverbed and breathed magic into them. She melted the stones together, and used this multicolored glass to repair the tear in the sky. She collected ash from burned reeds and built dams to block the floodwaters.

Finally, the gentle goddess took up Pan Gu's axe, and attacked Gong Gong for his many crimes. Long they battled, and Gong Gong was at first surprised, and then fearful, of Nü Wa's wrath, for he had never considered her a worthy opponent. His fangs and claws flashed and drew Nü Wa's blood, but it was her axe that found the mark, and she cleaved his head from his serpentine neck. At the sight of the blood-soaked goddess holding the head of Gong Gong in her hand, the demons that had invaded the world from the tear in the sky fled in terror.

Nü Wa's remaining people cheered and celebrated their survival, and began to rebuild their lives. It was

not so easy for the goddess. The great efforts she had expended to save her beloved creations had taxed her utterly. She lay down upon the earth, exhausted, and fell into a deep slumber.

When she opened her eyes she was in the celestial palace of the Jade Emperor, where she was received as a conquering hero, and given the best of care to aid her recovery from the injuries to her body and spirit.

Yet, Nü Wa's thoughts forever bend toward the people of earth, and she will always remain their staunchest defender.

Izanagi and Izanami

When the first divinities—known as Kami—came into being, they ruled the celestial paradise above, while below nothing existed but a primordial ocean. The Kami decided to bring life to this emptiness, so they created Izanagi-no-Mikoto (He who invites) and Izanami-no-Mikoto (She who invites) with the intention that they should descend from the heavens to create a new realm.

Izanagi and Izanami, clothed in shining garments, were eager to set upon their task. They joined hands and stepped upon the floating bridge of heaven. Gazing down, they could discern no solid land for them to step upon. At this they created a magnificent spear with an indestructible blade and a hardwood shaft studded with jewels. They threw the spear to the divine couple, who caught it deftly. Izanagi and Izanami pushed the heavenly jeweled spear into the water below and stirred its depths. The water churned and bubbled, and then they lifted up the spear. Its blade glistened with brine. They flicked the spear, and the brine flew onto the surface of the water and formed an island called Onogoro.

Izanagi and Izanami departed heaven and made Onogoro their home. Within a short time, the island flourished with plants and animals due to the efforts of the couple. They created a huge stone pillar, carved with the blessings of heaven, and placed it beside the beautiful hall where they lived. During this busy time, when they toiled side-by-side, delighting at their creations, they grew to love each other deeply. They decided to marry and they began their wedding preparations. They each created their costumes in private to surprise the other on their special day. On the morning of their nuptials, Izanagi walked around the pillar from the right, and Izanami walked from the left. When they met in the middle they cried out joyfully at their outfits: They wore kimonos fashioned from silk and brocade, and their elaborately coiffed hair shone glossy black in the sun. They made their vows under the pillar of heaven and returned to their home.

Yet, while they remained happy, they did not have any children. After a time they consulted the celestial Kami, who gave the couple instructions on how to repeat their

marriage ceremony with more solemnity, and less emphasis on their appearance. Izanagi and Izanami followed the ritual correctly, and in the following years Izanami gave birth to fourteen islands and dozens of Kami children, who were charged with the care of various animals, seasons, plants, and seas.

All was well until Izanami went into labor with Kagu-tsuchi, the Kami of Fire. The infant, unable to control his power, burned his mother terribly. Izanami, blackened and scorched, died, and from her smouldering body a number of other Kami came into existence.

It was the first time that death had entered this world, and the shock of it was too much for Izanagi. Crazed and weeping, he cried out to the heavens in pain, and clung to his dead wife's body. When he heard the mewling of his infant son, Izanagi became enraged, drew his sword, and cut off the head of the boy. From the splatters of blood that flew off Izanagi's sword, and dripped from his fingers, more Kami emerged. Kagu-tsuchi's blood drained from his small body into the clay, and from that mixture volcanoes sprang up across the islands. To this day, they erupt fire when the memory of the tragedy consumes them.

With a numb heart, Izanagi climbed to Mount Hiba and buried his wife so she could remain close to the heavens from whence she came.

Grief overwhelmed Izanagi. Nothing gladdened his heart, for everything he saw in the world prospered because of his union with Izanami. He could not imagine how the earth continued without her, but time restlessly moved on

while Izanagi remained stuck, buried in mourning. Finally, he decided he could not continue without his wife. He dressed in a black kimono and headdress, and embarked on a journey to Yomi-no-Kuni, the underworld—the realm of ghosts, restless spirits, pollution, and darkness.

Izanagi entered the gloom and hunted for Izanami. The cries of the dishonored rang in his ears, and the deranged pulled upon his garments. He brushed them off until he arrived at the castle, erected upon a great rock in the center of Yomi-no-Kuni, around which thousands of the dead crept and murmured. They all wore veils like dusty cobwebs, but Izanagi noticed Izanami's glorious eyes flash from behind her veil, and he ran to her.

"Izanami! Beloved, return with me to the land of the living. We have much more to do together."

Izanami clutched her veil close to her face, and her shoulders heaved with a sob. "Izanagi, I would dearly love to return with you, but I have eaten food from the hearth in the castle. I am forbidden to leave!"

For a time they held each other, until Izanami broke away, and whispered to her husband. "I will petition the Kami of this place and beg for release. Wait here and do not follow me."

Izanagi agreed, and he lingered among the crowds of the dead who forever marched and moaned under the winged eaves of the castle.

Izanagi had no way to reckon time's passage, but he grew tired of his dreary company, and wondered what kept his wife. In that dull and lifeless place, he could feel his heartbeat

> from her smouldering body a number of other Kami came into existence.

slow in response. Impatient and bored, Izanagi pushed his way through the dead bodies, and climbed up the winding path to enter the first gate of the fortress.

Inside the threshold he collided with his wife, who was hurrying to find him. Her veil slipped from her head. Izanagi looked upon her face, and stopped, startled by her visage. Her rotting skin hung from her bones, maggots crawled out of her gapping nose and toothless mouth; and her loose eyes glared up at him. Around her he could sense the Kami of Thunder gathering, attracted to her outrage.

"You have shamed me," she shrieked, and pulled the veil once again over her face. "Why did you not do as I asked?"

Blue sparks snapped around her body, and Izanagi felt the hair on his arms rising. He stepped backward, away from her, and that infuriated Izanami more.

She screamed the sound of pure betrayal. It penetrated the air, and woke the spirits of all the scorned and discarded women in Yomi-no-Kuni. Wailing, the horrid host flocked to her side, and their awful gazes condemned Izanagi.

He ran.

The cloud of ghost women pursued him closely, their hungry cries loud in his ears, and behind him ran Izanami, cursing him. Terrified, Izanagi threw off his headdress, and when it hit the ground it turned into grapes. The famished dead halted, and fell upon the food, devouring it. Izanagi dared glance behind him. The revenants had finished their meal and were back on his trail. As he sprinted toward the entrance, he grabbed the hair comb from his head, and flung it into the path. It instantly sprouted into bamboo cane, and once again the deceased stopped to eat it. Izanagi now gained an advantage, and at that moment Izanami summoned the Kami of Thunder, whose bellows deafened Izanagi and almost made him stumble. Along with them arose a thousand warriors, and they swept after Izanagi, swords drawn, shouting war cries.

Izanagi drew his sword, and swung it behind him as he ran, slicing through soldiers and Kami alike. He spotted the entrance to the living world, and sped forward. A peach tree grew by the opening, and when Izanagi ran into the daylight, he seized the peaches and pelted the dead with them—they paused to eat the fruit, and in that moment Izanagi heaved a huge boulder to block the entrance to Yomi-no-kuni.

He stood, panting, and heard his wife shout from behind the rock. "Izanagi, if you do this I will strangle a thousand people a day so they will depart your world, and reside with me in the land of the dead!"

Izanagi straightened up, and said in a clear voice, "And if you do that I will ensure that a thousand and five hundred people will be born every day."

Then silence came between the couple. A final hush that could never be breached.

Izanami placed her hand upon the rock in the darkness of Yomi-no-Kuni, and cried silently, grieving for the life she had lost. Then she returned to the castle, and began her reign as the Ruler of Yomi-no-Kuni.

Izanagi listened to the sounds of the dead departing, and he mourned his wife a final time.

Then, he turned around and noticed the wonderful vitality around him: the birds in the sky, the sun on the cherry blossom, and spring water tumbling over rocks.

Izanagi smiled and embraced the life that surrounded him.

Amaterasu Hides Her Face

When the god Izanagi left Yomi, the underworld, and accepted his eternal separation from his wife, Izanami, who had become ruler of that realm, he decided to purify his body and spirit. He removed his robes of mourning, scrubbed his skin with sand, and waded into a fresh pool of water. He ducked his head under the clear water, but its chill surprised him. Izanagi straightened quickly, shook his hair, and bellowed. Water flew from his mouth and eyes and three new Kami were born: Amaterasu, her brother Tsukuyomi, and their youngest brother, Susanoo.

Izanagi was pleased with his three offspring. There was no being as radiant as Amaterasu, so Izanagi decreed that she and her brother Tsukuyomi should climb the celestial ladder and live in the heavens where their luminous bodies would bring hope and life to the world below. Amaterasu became the shining sun, and Tsukuyomi the pale moon. For a time they were inseparable, and delighted in each other's company—which was good since neither of them found their intemperate younger brother, Susanoo, agreeable.

One day Amaterasu asked Tsukuyomi to accompany her to a meal with Uke Mochi, the goddess of bounty and food. Amaterasu sent her brother ahead while she finished dressing for the visit. Uke Mochi had the reputation for being a generous host, so Tsukuyomi walked to her home eagerly, looking forward to a feast. Uke Mochi greeted him pleasantly and escorted Tsukuyomi to a room where many doors slid open to the outside. One entrance looked over a beach, where the ocean waves crashed and swept the sand. Through another entrance, he saw trees that swayed in the forest. The view from the third entrance was of a rice paddy field. Tsukuyomi's stomach growled as he sat on his heels by the table, impatient for his meal.

Then, Uke Mochi did something odd: She picked up an empty bowl from the table, and glided to the doorway that overlooked the beach. She inhaled deeply, and spat a gleaming yellowtail fish into the dish. It flopped and expired before them. Tsukuyomi, revolted, almost jumped to his feet, but ingrained courtesy prevented him from following his instinct. Uke Mochi placed the bowl upon the table, picked up a long dish, and moved to face the forest. She began to cough and retch until a hunk of boar flesh was ejected from her mouth and onto the platter. This time Tsukuyomi could not restrain himself and leapt to his feet. Uke Mochi seemed oblivious to his discomfort. She laid the dish upon the table, and retrieved another bowl. Upon facing the paddy field, her shoulders began to heave. Tsukuyomi gritted his teeth to contain his rising nausea, and his hand crept to the hilt of his sword. His fingers tightened around it with every cough that came from Uke Mochi. After much noise, she regurgitated a heap of rice into the bowl.

Disgusted, and fighting the urge to vomit, Tsukuyomi unsheathed his sword and swung it at the goddess. His keen blade severed the head from her body. The spray of her blood across his face shocked him back to normal, and he stared at the corpse, horrified by his action. At that moment, he heard a soft cry: Amaterasu stood in the doorway with Uke Mochi's blood splashed across her favorite kimono.

She stared at Tsukuyomi with an expression of utter disbelief, slowly turned her back on her brother, and staggered from the room. From that point on Amaterasu refused to see her brother again no matter his plea or explanation. She kept to her part of the sky, and whenever he approached, she departed. Thus, the sun and moon were separated forever.

Amaterasu kept herself busy weaving and tending her fields, but without the company of Tsukuyomi she grew lonely. She found no comfort in Susanoo. Neither sibling got along with the other, and Susanoo seemed to delight in aggravating his older sister by playing cruel tricks on her at every opportunity. Susanoo also had a falling out with his father, Izanagi. The youngest son had been given dominion over the waters, but instead he wished to follow his mother into Yomi. Izanagi, afraid his son would become trapped in the underworld, insisted Susanoo take up his duties as god of seas and storms. As a result of this argument, Susanoo caused mischief throughout heaven, and vexed his family the most. Finally, Izanagi lost his temper and ordered his son to leave heaven and live in exile on earth. Susanoo angrily declared he didn't wish to live near his father anymore, and agreed to leave. But, he insisted upon seeing his sister a final time.

When Amaterasu heard the news, she picked up her bow and quiver of arrows to protect herself against her brother's temper, and met him at the agreed location in a clearing in the forest. Susanoo hailed his sister with suspicious charm, and claimed to wish to end the rivalry between them. He suggested they have a competition to set aside their differences and see which of them was truly the most powerful. Amaterasu quickly accepted the challenge, for she wished to teach her arrogant brother a lesson.

"Let us take an item from each other," Susanoo

suggested, "and whoever creates the most gods will win."

Amaterasu picked Susanoo's favorite sword, while Susanoo chose her necklace made from five jewels.

The goddess broke the sword into three pieces, and ate them. For a long time she munched and chewed on the pieces, and eventually exhaled a fine mist. It coalesced into the forms of three beautiful goddesses, who were *almost* as fair as Amaterasu. After witnessing this, Susanoo popped the jewels into his mouth and cracked them with this teeth. After a time he breathed out a fog, and from it five gods stepped forward who were *almost* as powerful as Susanoo.

At this, Susanoo leaped up and punched the air in delight, and claimed he had won since Amaterasu had produced only three goddesses. He danced around his sister being insufferable, and all her good will drained from her as he proved himself as ill-mannered as before.

"You are mistaken, dear brother," she said, interrupting his capering antics, "I have won. It was *my necklace* that produced five gods. Your sword could only evoke three goddesses."

Susanoo's face reddened with rage, but he could not refute his sister's logic. In his fury, he summoned a terrible storm. Black clouds rushed in, the winds bent the trees, and lightning struck the earth all around Amaterasu. She remained calm in the face of this provocation, for his tantrum could not erase her victory. Instead, she felt a pang of pity for his pettiness. Susanoo saw her expression change, and it infuriated him even more. He summoned a whirlwind and flew out of the clearing, destroying everything in his path.

He didn't depart the heavens as he had agreed, but remained hidden and began a campaign of harassment against his sister. Susanoo never confronted his sister openly, but needled her through myriad indirect methods.

One night, he crept into her rice fields and kicked down the divisions, filled up the irrigating channels, and opened the floodgate of the sluices to flood the fields at the wrong time. On another evening, he sowed inferior seeds among her crop, so the whole harvest was ruined. Amaterasu became exasperated by Susanoo's actions, but continued about her work, and ignored his taunts. This only incensed him further, and his actions grew crueler.

When the Autumn Harvest Festival neared, Amaterasu prepared a celebration for her workers and friends in recognition of their hard work and companionship. She decorated a hall with the bright red and orange colors of Japanese maple leaves, and she cooked a lavish banquet. When she departed to bring her guests to her feast, Susanoo blew the door open with lightning and summoned a gusting wind to strip the decorations and whip the food from the tables. He also used the squall to carry muck and excrement into the room where it was spread over the walls and the floor. Then he retired to a safe place to watch his sister's reaction.

Amaterasu returned with her cheerful group of finely dressed guests, but stopped, appalled, at the doorway of her feasting hall. Her friends fell silent, and tears gathered in Amaterasu's eyes. They tried to console her, and they organized a spontaneous picnic outdoors instead. It only heightened her embarrassment. Everyone suspected that Susanoo had defiled the festival to wound his sister. They whispered among themselves about his behavior, which only deepened Amaterasu's humiliation. Yet, she resolved to perk up, and after a time, she began to laugh with her friends again.

Her happiness grated on Susanoo's nerves. He pondered how to hurt his sister even more, and laid low for a while so Amaterasu would become less guarded. Several days later, Amaterasu gathered her female friends in her home and they spent a pleasant afternoon weaving and conversing. Susanoo gauged that the time was right for him to execute his next plan.

He found a colt, killed it, and flayed the skin from its body. He hung the fresh, bloody skin in the room of her home that she used as a shrine and sanctuary. Then, he kicked open the door to the goddess's room, and all the ladies looked up at him from their looms, startled. He flung the skinned corpse into the room among the graceful women, splattering them with gore. The ladies screamed, and one of them fainted at the shock—she

He pondered how to hurt his sister even more, and laid low for a while so Amaterasu would become less guarded.

thought Susanoo had thrown a human body at them.

Amaterasu bolted for her sanctuary, dragging her weeping friends along with her. When they opened the door they were horrified to see the peeled horse skin, hanging from the ceiling, dripping blood.

It was too much for Amaterasu: Her most private room had been violated. Fury at the indignity overtook her shock. She ran out of her home and into the wild, not knowing where she was going. After a long, ragged run through the trees she came to a cave. She walked inside, rolled a huge bolder in front of the entrance, and sat in blessed solitude. Her natural luminescence lit the space with a soft glow. Since Amaterasu was a goddess, she could remain in the cave in peace and quiet for as long as she wished. She let out a long breath, relaxed, and decided to stay.

Without Amaterasu in the heavens, the world was plunged into darkness. Panic erupted among the humans and the gods, for Tsukuyomi's light was a pale reflection of his sister's. Everyone needed torches to see, the crops withered, and the animals and birds became confused. People could not feed themselves. Evil gods and spirits emerged from their festering hideaways, and began plaguing the dispirited people of the world. All was hopeless and black.

The gods began a frantic search for the missing sun goddess. When they finally located her, the eight hundred gods gathered near the stoppered cave and pleaded for

her to return her light to the world. Her father cajoled her at first, and explained that Susanoo had been thrown from the heavens down to earth for his terrible insults to Amaterasu. After a time he became stern, and ordered her to return to her duty and shine in the heavens once more. Amaterasu did not reply or come out.

The only goddess who had not despaired of a solution was Ama-no-Uzume, who laughed easily and saw joy and humor even during the most difficult dilemmas. She knew Amaterasu well, and guessed the goddess would not be able to resist a mystery. She instructed the other gods to bring a large mirror and place it in front of the cave, and they hung it with pearls and jewels. Ama-no-Uzume also asked them to bring many roosters to the cave, and let them loose. The gods were puzzled by these strange requests, but Ama-no-Uzume's optimism in the face of despair encouraged them to fulfill her requests.

She ordered a sacred fire to be built before the cave, stripped off her clothes, and dressed herself in garlands of moss and strings of bamboo leaves. Then she overturned a tub, and stood on top of it in front of her fellow gods and goddesses. In one hand she held a branch with tinkling bells. She began to dance in a comical fashion, her feet thrumming a beat on the tub, and her bells chiming along foolishly. Soon her audience were clapping along with the beat and roaring with laughter. They forgot about Amaterasu and their problems, and embraced the joy of Ama-no-Uzume's dance.

Amaterasu pressed her ear against the boulder blocking the cave, and tried to figure out what was happening outside. She heard the rhythm of the beat and the laughter, and wondered why no one begged for her return anymore. She slowly rolled the boulder back a little so she could peer outside. All the roosters

immediately cried out to herald the return of the sun, and the gods turned to gaze upon the luminous visage of Amaterasu. The first thing the goddess saw was her own blinding reflection in the mirror strung with jewels. In that moment, she fully appreciated her true nature and her glory. She was not someone who hid away from difficulty—she was a goddess who shone through any problem! The gods gathered around her and begged that she return to her divine position in the heavens. She readily agreed.

Finally, they asked her to swear never to hide her face from gods or humans ever again. In response, Amaterasu hooked her arm through the crook of Ama-no-Uzume's arm, and they spun together, dancing and laughing. The gods stamped their feet and applauded, and the world celebrated the return of the sun to the skies.

Exiled on earth, Susanoo heard the merriment of the gods, and gazed up at the return of his sister's radiance in the sky. The gods had exacted a harsh punishment on Susanoo before they cast him from their court. In their fury at his despicable behavior, a gang of them had surrounded him and torn his beard off, while others ripped off his finger and toenails. It was only the intercession of his father, Izanagi, that prevented more serious torture. Instead, he ordered his son tossed from the high heavens. Susanoo plummeted to earth and crashed into a valley, bloodied and bruised.

Despite his pain, Susanoo smiled at the sight of Amaterasu's bright presence. He had suffered in the darkness on earth, desperate and alone, hearing the distant cries of those being tormented by demons and terrible spirits. During those black days and nights all Susanoo could do was ponder his actions, and regret and guilt entered his heart. With Amaterasu's return,

Susanoo realized how awful the world, and his life, had been without his sister. He did not know how he could make amends, or if anything he ever did again would obtain his sister and father's forgiveness, but Susanoo decided he would strive to prove himself a better god.

He limped to the bank of the River Hi so he could drink water and wash his wounds. After he finished his ablutions, he cleaned his sword, and began to feel almost civilized. At that moment, he heard a faint keening in the distance. Susanoo stood up, adjusted his clothing so he looked presentable, and marched toward the sound. He came to a pretty, orderly building with an ornate garden. A pregnant woman sat hunched on a stone bench by a pool in which brightly colored koi fish swam. Her tears splashed into the water, and by her side, a man comforted her.

Susanoo hailed them courteously, but the couple barely took note of the stranger's arrival.

"May I be of service?" he asked.

They only shook their heads at first, until he coaxed them to divulge the reason for their sorrow. They explained that they were the god Ashinazuchi, son of the god of the mountain, and Tenazuchi, daughter of the goddess of the river. This was Tenauzuchi's eighth pregnancy, but their previous seven daughters had all been consumed upon birth by a giant eight-headed monster named Yamata no Orochi. The parents grieved because they feared the same

fate would befall their latest child.

Susanoo swore he would not allow this to happen, and the light of hope entered the couple's eyes. "Describe to me this creature," he said.

Ashinazuchi replied, "Most fearsome is that it has eight heads, and each one has a pair of eyes as red as ripened cherries, and teeth as sharp as the finest sword. It also has eight arms, a serpent's body, and eight tails. It is so huge, firs and cypresses grow from its back, and if its entire length was laid out straight it would occupy eight valleys and eight hills."

Susanoo pondered the problem and a risky solution came to mind. "Come, we have much to do," he told the couple. He instructed them to gather all the fruits they had available and to brew eight jars of intoxicating sake. Once that was done, they constructed a huge fence in front of the house that had eight gates. Behind each gate was a small platform, and upon each platform they placed a jar of strong sake.

Just as their tasks were accomplished, Tenazuchi felt the pain of labor, and Ashinazuchi and Susanoo helped her into the house. Many hours later, a baby girl was born, and the couple named her Kushinada-hime. As soon as the baby wailed another sound was heard: the terrible bellows of Yamata no Orochi. Susanoo stopped sharpening his sword, and left the house to wait for the arrival of the beast. Tenazuchi cradled her child to her breast and rocked it, while Ashinazuchi guarded the door.

The massive, eight-headed creature slithered up to the house confident it had another feast waiting, but was surprised to discover the large fence and gates blocking its way. Its eight pairs of blood-red eyes narrowed when it saw Susanoo standing in front of the fence.

The god bowed low. "Mighty Yamata no Orochi," he said, "in respect of your reputation I have prepared a welcome drink for you."

The monster's noses sniffed and smelled the sake. It inserted each of its heads through a gate, and Susanoo ran from head to head and poured the jar of sake into each mouth. The drink was so potent that within moments of consuming all eight jars, Yamata no Orochi fell asleep. Its snores shook the ground.

Susanoo didn't hesitate: He chopped off each of Yamata no Orochi's heads, and didn't stop there. He also lopped of each of its tails, and there was so much blood it dyed the River Hi red for weeks.

While Susanoo was cutting off the fourth tail, his sword became notched. He frowned, annoyed at the damage to his weapon, but also curious as to what could cause such a dent. He slit open the tail and inside it lay the finest sword Susanoo ever beheld. Instantly he named it *Ame-no-Murakumo-no-Tsurugi*—the Sword of the Gathering Clouds of Heaven. He decided he would give the sword to his sister Amaterasu as a gift, as a way to end the rift between them.

He slit open the tail and inside it lay the finest sword Susanoo ever beheld.

Yet, Amaterasu did not trust her brother, and turned away all envoys from him. Susanoo decided to rebuild her trust, and continued to help those who were struggling or in difficulty. Many years passed, and Amaterasu watched her brother from the skies and observed his change in character. Slowly, as Amaterasu witnessed his many good deeds, she let go of her old resentments. She began to evaluate her brother anew based on his current actions, and not his past mistakes. It was not easy for the goddess to relinquish her grudge after all the tricks and cruelty Susanoo had heaped upon her, but through time and the evidence of Susanoo's reform, she finally eased it from her grasp.

Susanoo became good friends with Ashinazuchi and Tenazuchi, and visited them often. Their daughter, Kushinada-hime, grew up quickly and became a beautiful, accomplished goddess. Over time she fell in love with Susanoo, and began to attract his attention. Her parents were pleased with the match, for they had only ever known Susanoo as a courageous, giving god, and they believed he would be a worthy husband for their daughter.

After a long courtship, Susanoo and Kushinada-hime decided to marry, and began their wedding preparations. While everyone else planned the details with excitement, Susanoo seemed less enthusiastic. After gentle questioning, Kushinada-hime managed to elicit the reason from Susanoo: None of his family would be at the wedding. Susanoo had confided to Kushinada-hime the mistakes of his past before he proposed, and it had made Kushinada-hime pause to re-consider what she knew of Susanoo. In the end, she decided to accept Susanoo as the brave and caring god she had always known, but also to appreciate that his current state of grace had manifested because of his former lapses in judgement.

Kushinada-hime sent a personal messenger to Amaterasu with a long letter, detailing her understanding of the rift between the siblings, along with her wish that her wedding to Susanoo could start the healing of that old hurt. The sun goddess sat with the note for a long time, pondered all that had occurred in recent years, and gazed down upon the earth and at her brother.

On the day of the marriage of Susanoo and Kushinada-hime, Amaterasu and Izanagi descended from the heavens to attend the ceremony and celebrations. Overjoyed, Susanoo presented Amaterasu with *Ame-no-Murakumo-no-Tsurugi* as a gift upon their reconciliation. The goddess accepted it with pleasure, for there was no mightier sword on heaven or on earth, and it was a sure sign of Susanoo's commitment to change. Previously, he would have guarded such a treasure jealously and refused to bestow it upon another. Izanagi and Susanoo

also reunited, and Izanagi acknowledged that Susanoo could venture where he wished, and if Susanoo wanted to journey to Yomi, it was his right to do so.

It was a happy day on earth and the heavens, for Susanoo and Kushinada-hime's wedding not only celebrated their love, but also repaired the bonds of affection between Susanoo, Amaterasu, and Izanagi. From that point onward if Amaterasu and Susanoo ever bickered, they always forgave each other once their tempers cooled.

Storm clouds do not obscure the sun forever, even if it seems like they blacken the sky endlessly. They eventually calm and clear, and her light always returns to brighten the world once more.

Monkey: Sage of Heaven

The magnificent Flower Fruit Mountain, in the kingdom of Aolai, basked in nature's elements for millions of years. Sun, moon, rain, and wind were its companions, and down in the forest coating the steep sides of its base lived a rambunctious tribe of monkeys. The mountain gestated these influences, and gave birth to a stone egg at its peak. The sun warmed the egg, the moon silvered it, the rain cleaned its pitted surface, and the wind tapped on its shell. One day it cracked open, and from it sprang a stone monkey, flexible in form and irrepressible in spirit. His first act was to bow to the four directions, and at this, his eyes shot golden lightning into the heavens, and illuminated the Palace of the North Star.

Brimming with the powers of nature, bursting with curiosity for the world, the monkey charged down the mountain, eager to learn all that there was to know. He swung through the trees, gobbled fruits, dashed through rivers, leaped over rocks, teased tigers, soared alongside cranes, loped with wolves, and made friends with everyone. The other monkeys of the mountain, impressed by his outrageous exploits and fine demeanor, named him Handsome Monkey King.

He led the troop of monkeys to a cave hidden behind a waterfall, so they were safe from predators and sheltered from the elements. For hundreds of years they were happy. Over time, he became troubled by death. He watched other members of his adopted family fade and die, and it saddened him.

One of Monkey's courtiers noticed his sorrow, and upon discovering its reason, said, "There are only three types exempt from the touch of Yama, King of Death: Buddhas, immortals, and sages." Monkey instantly decided to embark upon a quest to become immortal. He waved goodbye to his friends in Water Curtain Cave, and bounded into the wider world, eager to learn more about its ways and customs.

For a decade, he traveled over land and sea, and discovered humans. He learned to speak their language and wear human garments—his favorite outfit was a scarlet gown with a yellow silk sash, and black boots. All the time he searched for a wise person who could instruct him, but most men and women he met were only interested in mundane matters. Finally, in the Cave of the Setting Moon and Three Stars, high up on the mountain Ling Fang Zhun Shan, the immortal sage Subhuti accepted Monkey as his pupil. He gave Monkey the name Sun Wukong, and for twenty years Monkey toiled under Master Subhuti's tutelage.

At first, Monkey was only allowed to sweep the grounds, hoe weeds, cut wood, and carry water as a test of his character. These were all new things to Monkey, so he performed them well, not seeing the humility the tasks were supposed to engender. Soon, he was also reading scriptures, practicing calligraphy, discussing philosophy, and learning to behave properly. In time, Master Subhuti rewarded Monkey's diligence by teaching him almost all of his secrets, including the seventy-two magical transformations, how to create replicas of himself from his hair, the art of riding across the sky on a cloud, and a leap called *jindouyun* that could carry him 108,000 li (33,550 miles).

Proud of his new skills, Monkey began showing off to the other disciples, who encouraged him in his antics —not that Monkey required much prompting. Monkey bounced around on the clouds, and transformed into whatever his fellow students asked. Within a short time they were clapping and laughing, and causing quite a disturbance, which disturbed Master Subhuti.

The revered sage left his room to investigate, and witnessed Monkey's pride and foolishness. He recognized that Monkey's nature was still too raw and preoccupied with self, so he banished Monkey from the temple. Monkey accepted his punishment with sadness, and using his new powers leaped back to Water Curtain Cave in no time. When he landed near the waterfall, his followers rushed out of the trees to meet him. They were ecstatic at his return, but he noticed their numbers had diminished and they were weary.

He asked the reason why, and they told him, "Your Majesty, the Demon of Havoc besieged our cave and ran us out of it. He lives to the north and appears in mist and lightning, and disappears in the same fashion. Lately, he has been stealing our children, and we must be vigilant at all times to protect our young."

Incensed, Monkey leaped the huge distance northward to land by the entrance to Demon's home in a mountain. Monkey ran up to the lesser demons guarding the doorway and demanded to see their master. They scurried down the tunnel to the Demon of Havoc's throne room, and reported that Handsome Monkey King was outside and shouting for revenge.

The Demon of Havoc laughed when he heard Monkey was unarmed. He dressed in armor, grabbed his huge sword, and stamped out to meet the impetuous

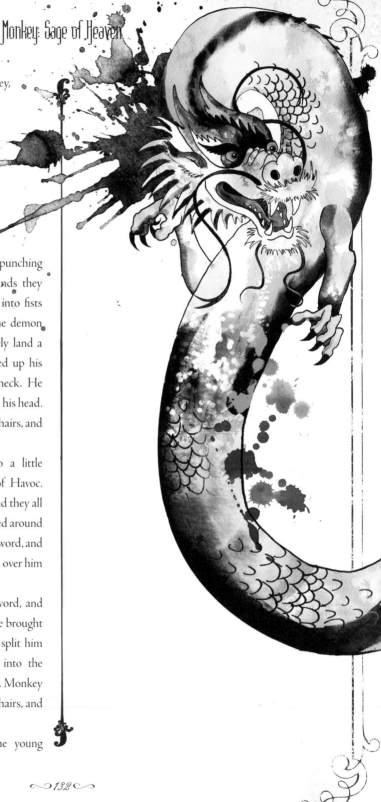

beast. The Demon towered over Monkey, and roared, "Diminutive rogue, you dare challenge me?"

Monkey raised his fists. "Insolent demon! I could pull the moon down from the sky if I wished! Prepare yourself!"

The demon flung down his sword. "I'll knock off your conceited head!"

Monkey dashed at the demon, kicking and punching with furious speed. When he spread his hands they became enormous, when he tightened them into fists they were diamond-hard. Within minutes, the demon was bruised and bleeding, and he could barely land a blow on Monkey. Enraged, the demon picked up his massive sword and swung it at Monkey's neck. He ducked, and its passage swept the hairs back on his head. At this he smiled. He pulled out several of his hairs, and cried out "change!"

Immediately, each hair transformed into a little monkey, and they barreled at the Demon of Havoc. Monkey King plucked out more of his hairs and they all became small versions of himself. They swarmed around the demon, nimbly avoiding each swipe of his sword, and hit, tripped, and kicked him, before climbing all over him and beating him badly.

Monkey seized the Demon of Havoc's sword, and yelled at his monkeys to get out of the way. He brought down the sword on the demon's crown, and split him in half. Then he and his retinue sprinted into the mountain and killed all the remaining demons. Monkey transformed the small monkeys back into his hairs, and put them back on his body.

He discovered the prison where all the young

monkeys from Water Curtain Cave had been kept, and released them. He uttered a spell and summoned a hurricane to return the monkey children home, while he rode along with them on a cloud with the demon's sword in his hand.

After this adventure Monkey trained his people every day to fight. He raided a nearby town for an array of weapons, and taught his monkey army how to use them.

Within months, all the regions in the area paid tribute to the Monkey King, and none dared attack him.

Yet, Monkey was dissatisfied with every weapon he used, even the demon's sword. He asked his advisors where he could find a weapon worthy of his skill.

They told him to follow the stream under the iron bridge, which would lead him to the palace of Ao Guang, the Dragon King of the Eastern Sea. "You are certain to find an appropriate weapon among his vast treasure trove."

Monkey, versed in many spells, cast one to allow him to breathe under water, and he swam deep into the Eastern Sea until he came to the coral palace of the Dragon King. When he heard of Monkey's arrival, Ao Guang came out to greet him, along with his dragon children and the company of crab generals and prawn soldiers.

After introductions, they settled in the Dragon's throne room, and Monkey made his request. "I require a weapon of the best quality, and I am informed that you possess so many you would hardly miss one."

Monkey's reputation had preceded him, and Ao Guang did not want to offend his guest. He gestured to a servant, and within moments they returned with a finely crafted sword. Monkey frowned and crossed his arms. "I don't like swords," he said.

The Dragon King nodded, and another weapon was displayed—a nine-pronged spear so heavy it took a dozen servants to carry it. Monkey lifted it easily. "Too light," he said, dismissive. Startled, Ao Guang asked for another one to be brought forward. This time it was a magical halberd that warded off spells and weighed over seven thousand pounds. Monkey pursed his lips and whirled the weapon a couple of times as if it was a stick of wood. He sniffed. "No good. Surely a King of your reputation must own a better weapon?"

The Dragon King was quite alarmed at Monkey's prowess. His wife noticed, and whispered in his ear that he should offer Monkey *Ruyi Jingu Bang*, the immense iron rod that no one could lift.

Ao Guang showed Monkey into the middle of his treasury where *Ruyi Jingu Bang* stood—an enormous black iron pillar, banded on both ends in gold. At Monkey's appearance, it shone like the blazing midday sun. Monkey laid his hands on its surface, and said, "If only it was smaller, so I could test its ability."

At that, the iron rod shrunk to the size of a pole, and Monkey laughed in pleasure. The Dragon and his entourage were silent in terror as Monkey twirled the rod around him striking various poses. The rod could break bones just by brushing past the skin of a creature.

Smiling with glee, Monkey wondered aloud if it could shrink to the size of a needle, and the rod became so small that Monkey could tuck it behind his ear.

Ao Guang, hoping his guest was satisfied, tried to move him out of his treasury.

"Just one more thing," said Monkey, "I need armor to match this wonderful weapon. I'm sure you won't disappoint me." He ordered the rod back to the size of a pole, and leaned against it nonchalantly.

Ao Guang summoned his three brothers, Ao Qin, the Dragon King of the Southern Sea, Ao Shun, the Dragon King of the Northern Sea, and Ao Run, the Dragon King of the Western Sea, and asked them to donate armor to Monkey. They were livid at the request, but when they discovered Monkey possessed *Ruyi Jingu Bang* they relented. The four dragon brothers decided to send complaints to the Emperor of Heaven about Monkey's behavior once he had departed.

They gave Monkey a pair of cloud walking shoes, a suit of golden chain mail, and a phoenix feathered helmet. Monkey accepted their gifts, and put them on. He thanked the Dragon Kings, shot away from the palace, and burst out of the water, glittering in the sun.

His people were awed by his outfit and weapon, and

put on a lavish banquet, with singing and drumming, to celebrate his achievements. Monkey indulged himself, and slept deeply that night after an abundance of rich foods and wine.

Later on, as he slept, two men appeared, one of them holding a piece of paper that read "Sun Wukong". They captured Monkey's soul, and dragged him to a vast city surrounded by a gigantic wall. Monkey spotted an iron plaque attached to the wall by rivets. On it was inscribed "World of Darkness," and Monkey sobered up quickly—he was being brought to the realm of the dead.

He spoke to his captors, "This is where King Yama resides. I am not under his jurisdiction! Release me."

One of the men grunted, as if he had heard this argument before. "Your life is over if we are ordered to fetch you."

Monkey lost his temper, and pulled the tiny rod from behind his ear. He commanded it to grow, and knocked out the two servants. Monkey slipped out of his bonds, and rushed into the city, swinging his *Ruyi Jingu Bang*, and scattering all who crossed his path. Many of them rushed to Senluo Palace and cried out for help from the Ten Kings who sit in judgement of the deceased.

The Kings were afraid, for no mortal could attack the city in this fashion. They stepped out into the street to meet the intruder, and stopped suddenly when they saw his attacks and ferocious expression. "What is your name, exulted immortal?" They asked.

Monkey halted his rampage, and glared at them. "If you don't know my name, why am I here?"

"Help us clear up this matter."

"I am Sun Wukong, the King of the Water Curtain Cave on Flower Fruit Mountain."

"Ah," they said, "No doubt our servants brought the wrong person."

Monkey banged his iron rod on the ground and a crevice opened up along the street. "Take me to the Register of Life and Death so I might see how this blunder occurred."

The kings bowed, and hurried to the Senluo Palace with Monkey following them. They ordered the large registers brought forth, and after much searching found the entry: "Soul No. 1350—Sun Wukong, the stone monkey. He will die at age 342."

"Nonsense!" Monkey declared. "I have gone beyond the Three Worlds, and am no longer subject to the Five Elements. Get me ink and a brush."

When the implements arrived, Monkey crossed out his name, and also crossed out all the names under the monkey section. He threw the huge tome on the floor.

"We are no longer subject to your control." With that, he took off and whipped his iron rod at anyone who tried to bar his way. He beat his way out of the city and suddenly his generals were shaking Monkey awake.

> Monkey banged his iron rod on the ground and a crevice opened up along the street.

Monkey told his story to his people, and they praised him for helping them elude death.

That was not the end of the matter, for Monkey had changed the balance, and upset too many important people. The Ten Kings made a formal complaint to the Jade Emperor, who sits in the Golden Palace in the azure vault of Heaven. It was one of many complaints filed against the Monkey King, and at this point the Emperor believed something had to be done. His advisors suggested that instead of summoning the celestial armies to destroy Monkey, they should instead offer him a position in Heaven, which would appeal to Monkey's pride.

A divine envoy flew down with the offer to Monkey, who was pleased at the honor of a position in the heavenly household. He hopped on his cloud and flew up to heaven before the envoy, and almost started a fight when the guardians of heaven didn't recognize him. The envoy smoothed over the misunderstanding, and brought Monkey before the Jade Emperor.

He was given the title of "Protector of the Horses" at the Imperial Stables, and attended to his duties conscientiously. The Imperial horses were well fed and groomed at all times. When Monkey discovered that his position was considered a low grade, with no reward, he flew into a tantrum and departed heaven. His family and armies were happy he returned, and one of them suggested that he should have been given the title "Great

Sage Equalling Heaven." Monkey loved the idea, and had a banner made with that title upon it. He hung it above his throne.

In heaven, word got out that Monkey had abandoned his position, and the generals of heaven begged the Jade Emperor's permission to go to earth and chastise Monkey for his arrogance. The Emperor, fed up with placating Monkey, agreed to their plan.

General after general departed heaven believing he could defeat Monkey, but Sun Wukong bested them all.

When Monkey stepped out against an enemy resplendent in his golden armor, cloud-walking shoes, shining helmet, and bearing the iron rod, with the ability to transform himself and cast powerful spells, none could stand against him.

In the end the Jade Emperor called Monkey to heaven and granted him the title of "Great Sage Equalling Heaven." Appeased, Monkey accepted the title and enjoyed the prestige it gave him among the other immortals and gods. The decree did nothing to assuage Monkey's appetite for mischief, however. Within a short time of living in heaven, he had eaten most of the peaches of longevity in the Imperial Orchard, stolen jade liquor for his monkey family on earth, disrupted a grand banquet, and quit heaven out of boredom.

Furious, the Jade Emperor ordered all the generals and armies of heaven to attack and subdue Monkey

> Monkey told his story to his people, and they praised him for helping them elude death.

for his crimes. Monkey summoned his vassals and their armies, and wielding his powerful iron rod, he destroyed all the forces that assembled against him. Every trick they tried to use against Monkey failed, and this only incensed him further. In a great battle in the Hall of the Miraculous Mist in heaven, Monkey transformed to have three heads and six arms, and in each hand was a replica of his unstoppable iron rod. The firmament quaked from the destruction being wrought.

In desperation, the Jade Emperor sent a message to the Thunder Monastery in which Buddha resided, asking for his help. Buddha agreed, and he traveled instantly to the Hall where the armies of heaven were fighting the three-headed, six-armed Monkey King.

He called for the battle to end, and the hosts of heaven laid down their arms. Monkey returned to his usual form, and frowned at Buddha. "Who are you to tell me to stop?"

"I am Venerable Sakyamuni from the Western Land of Perfect Bliss," Buddha replied with a smile. "Your rebellion against heaven is over, and now you must surrender."

"I'll stop fighting," replied Monkey, "if the Jade Emperor abdicates and gives his throne to me."

The Buddha laughed. "Foolish Monkey. So you have magic and a fine weapon. That does not entitle you to rule heaven, which requires millennia of training."

Monkey bridled at that, and shouted, "I will continue to harass the Emperor so he will never rest easy again.

"How about a wager?" The Buddha stretched out his hand and said, "If you can somersault out of my palm, I will persuade the Jade Emperor to return with me and give you his palace."

Sun Wukong shrank immediately and in a streak of light he leaped into the center of Buddha's palm, certain of his ability to perform the feat. He made his great somersault and as he arced forward he saw five pink pillars rising up, which he took to be the pillars of heaven. When he landed by them he decided to mark one of them as evidence.

He wrote "The Great Sage Equalling Heaven Was Here," on the middle pillar. He somersaulted back to where he began, standing in the middle of Buddha's palm.

"That was too easy," bragged Monkey. "Name me Jade Emperor."

"You never left my palm." Buddha spread his fingers, and written on the middle finger was Monkey's note. The ink wasn't dry.

"What trick is this?" shouted Monkey, "I wrote on one of the pillars of heaven!" He braced himself to leap away again, but Buddha turned his hand over and pushed the Monkey King out of the Western Gate of Heaven. His five fingers became a mountain chain belonging to the elements Metal, Wood, Water, Fire, and Earth. He named it the Five Elements Mountain, and it pinned Monkey to the ground.

The Jade Emperor and his household celebrated with

the Buddha that evening, and later on, one of the guards reported that Monkey had managed to poke his head out from the mountain.

"No matter," said Buddha. He wrote a spell on a slip of paper. A servant posted it on top of the mountain peak, and it magically bound Monkey in place along with the tremendous weight of the mountain.

Later on, after the feasting, Buddha departed the gates of Heaven and gazed upon Monkey trapped under his rocky jail. He recited a spell, and set the gods to live upon the mountain range to watch over Monkey. They were instructed to feed him iron pellets when he was hungry, and pour molten copper into his mouth when he was thirsty.

Buddha paused to gaze upon Monkey. "When your punishment is over you will have the chance to redeem

yourself. I foresee many more adventures for you, but for now you must reflect upon your deeds."

Monkey railed and shouted, but he could not escape the trap. His meals and drinks were torture, and confined under the mountain, he could only ponder what brought him there—and plan how he would settle scores once he was free.

The Voice, The Flood, and The Turtle

Many years ago a tribe of the Caddo people lived in a large village in a valley overshadowed by the mighty Quachita Mountains and nourished by the Red River. Their Chief, Nin-tse, was a wise man, but he and his wife, Yun-noot, desperately wanted children. At night, when her husband slept, Yun-noot cried in the darkness and prayed to conceive.

At last, Yun-noot became pregnant, and her belly swelled to an enormous size. "She will have twins," some of her friends speculated. As she grew bigger they revised their guess to triplets. When Yun-noot went into labor she delivered four boys—but they were all strangely shaped.

The Elders of the village gathered in council to listen to the women who had aided Yun-noot during childbirth. "The babies are too large, they already have teeth, and each one has four legs and four arms." Many at that meeting argued that the babies should be killed for the safety of the tribe. They summoned Yun-noot, and told her their concerns. She stood before them, ashen from the ordeal of childbirth, and refused to believe that her children were

a threat. "They will grow up to be fine men just like their father. They will make our village proud," she insisted. Chief Nin-tse remained silent throughout the discussion. Yun-noot's passion and love persuaded the council, and they agreed that with such good parents the children would become valuable members of their tribe, no matter their appearance.

Yet, within each of the boys resided a malevolent spirit. They grew quickly, much faster than normal, and constantly caused trouble. Yun-noot always defended them, claiming they were boisterous when others called them ill-mannered, and saying that they were brave when others referred to them as cruel. The other children of the village learned to avoid the four bullies, who always walked together, or they would end up bruised and crying. Their mothers complained to Yun-noot, but she brushed it off as the normal fights between children.

Over time, as the boys grew as large as men, their disruptive nature and bad behavior destroyed the calm of the village. They were afraid of no one, and derided

those who tried to make peace with them. Nishkú'ntu, the village medicine man, could see their wicked natures clearly, and advised the council to kill them before they became too strong. Yet again, Yun-noot swayed the council with her assurances, and her subtle reminders that her husband was their chief.

After the council agreed not to take action against the four brothers, the young men of the village decided secretly to punish the brothers for their brutality. They ambushed the brothers one afternoon, and descended upon them, yelling and swinging wooden tomahawks. The brothers roared with laughter at the attack. They danced easily around their foes on their extra legs. Each of them could wield a bow and arrow with one pair of arms while hacking at their assailants with two tomahawks with the other pair. They fought like demons, and battered anyone in their reach. By the end of the skirmish two of the villagers lay dead. To the horror of the survivors, the brothers began carving strips of flesh off the deceased. They gnawed upon the meat, and blood stained their mouths. They lifted up their heads and howled in pleasure. In that terrible moment, the witnesses realized that the boys' true character had emerged. They ran back to the village to warn everyone.

The four brothers started growing soon after their meal. By the time they stomped into the center of the village, they towered over the tallest tribe member. They

> They ambushed the brothers one afternoon, and descended upon them, yelling and swinging wooden tomahawks.

stood back-to-back with their arms linked: one facing east, one facing south, one facing west, and one facing north. Their backs merged until they became one huge monster. With their sixteen arms, they grabbed people and snapped their necks. They ate the bodies, and after each corpse, the monster grew larger. Yun-noot ran out, pleading for them to stop. One of them raised a huge foot and crushed her. Chief Nin-tse screamed and fired arrows at his sons, but they bounced off their skin. One of their massive fists killed him with a single blow.

Soon they were taller than the mountains, and the remaining villagers hid among their giant feet, as it was impossible for them to bend down. The villages farther away were not so fortunate because the monster's arms could stretch great distances, and the brothers were always hungry. Their bodies grew ever taller, until their heads broke through the clouds and touched the sky.

At this point Nishkú'ntu heard a calm voice near his ear. "Plant a reed in the earth," it whispered, "and you will be saved."

Nishkú'ntu told his wife Cho-ah what he had heard, and she dashed to their home where she kept a supply of reeds. She returned and they ran a great distance outside the village until they came to soft, wet earth. The roars of the giant brothers above shook the ground. Nishkú'ntu knelt and carefully planted the reed. Within moments it sprouted, and grew until it was a huge tower in the sky. Its top pierced the clouds and touched the heavens.

Nishkú'ntu heard the voice again. It said, "I will send a flood into the world. When you see my sign, both of you must climb into this reed, naked as the moment you were born, and bring with you a pair of all the animals in the world."

"What will be your sign?" asked Nishkú'ntu.

"A huge flock, made up of birds of the woods, sea, deserts, and mountains. When you see this flock fly from north to south, you must come to this reed."

Nishkú'ntu and Cho-ah returned to their home near the feet of the monster, and began gathering pairs of animals. The creatures came to the couple eagerly, as if they were aware of what was to come. The monstrous brothers stamped their feet regularly, shaking the earth, and always stretching their long arms across the world to capture and eat people.

One morning Nishkú'ntu looked up and spotted a marvelous flock of birds form a huge shadow in the sky, flying from north to south.

He called to Cho-ah, and they gathered the animals in a line, and directed them to the colossal reed. Then they shed their clothes, and made their way into the reed. Inside was a long, circular ramp. They coaxed the beasts into the reed, and sealed up the entrance.

It began to rain.

They climbed steadily upward with the animals. They didn't have any food, but they did not feel hungry.

Outside the rain pounded, but no water fell into the reed. For days they traveled toward the tiny dot of light above them to the sound of gurgling water. Eventually the disc of light became bigger, and one day they stood at the top of the reed. All was blue and quiet, with just a soft breeze. In the distance they could see the huge scarlet faces of the four brothers. Below the top of the reed, the water churned against its side, just as it swirled around the necks of the brothers. The massive reed swayed with the water's currents, bending to its force, but not breaking.

One of the brothers complained loudly, "My legs are growing weary! The water is pushing me off-balance." His brothers urged him to be strong, and they dug their feet deeper into the mud below, but the water rose to their chins.

The voice spoke to Nishkú'ntu: "Now I shall send the Turtle to destroy the monstrous brothers."

Below the flood water, the Great Turtle swam to where the feet of the giant brothers were rooted in the mud. Using its strong limbs it uncovered their feet, and they could no longer stand firm. In their attempt to keep their heads above the water they broke apart, and without their unity they toppled over. They were washed into the roiling waters. One sank toward the north, one toward the east, one toward the south, and one toward the west, and so the four directions were forged.

After the monsters drowned, the waters began to recede. The tops of the mountains emerged first, followed by the hills, and then the rest of the land. Storm winds lashed the world and dried the earth.

Nishkú'ntu, Cho-ah, and all the animals climbed down for days, and opened the hole at the foot of the reed. They peered outside: Everything was dry.

They walked out of the reed, and discovered a desolate world. Once they were all outside, the reed collapsed and disappeared and the animals scattered and went their separate ways.

Cho-ah cried, thinking of her family and friends who had died. She said: "Nishkú'ntu, we're naked, and there's nothing left. How will we live?"

"Let us sleep. Tomorrow we will consider the problem anew."

So they lay down on the hard ground together, and slept.

The next morning they woke up and discovered that a variety of herbs had sprung up around them. There was enough to still their hunger for a day.

At daybreak the following morning they cried out in happiness: Trees and bushes grew everywhere. They gathered firewood, and set a fire to warm themselves. Nishkú'ntu began to make a bow and arrows.

After the third night, grass covered the earth, and animals appeared to graze on it.

Nishkú'ntu and Cho-ah went to sleep on the fourth night and woke up inside a large beehive-shaped, thatched hut. At the threshold of their home lay a stalk of corn.

The voice spoke, and both of them heard it: "This will be your holy food." It told them how to plant and harvest the corn, and said, "You have everything you need to live. Your children will be a new generation. If you ever plant corn, and something other than corn grows, then you know that the world has reached its true ending."

After that they never heard the voice again, but Nishkú'ntu and Cho-ah lived a long and happy life. Their children, and their children's children, spread across the green and fertile world, thankful for its bounty.